HYBRID

A NOVEL BY MICHAEL COLE

SEVERED PRESS
HOBART TASMANIA

HYBRID

Copyright © 2020 MICHAEL COLE

WWW.SEVEREDPRESS.COM

ISBN: 978-1-922323-91-0

CHAPTER 1

"Where am I?"

The man was speaking to himself, but he suspected he was being heard.

"Why did you bring me here?"

The room was dark except for a white light illuminating from a twelve-inch video monitor. That light glinted from the rectangular lenses of the scientist that watched. Other than that, the room was coated in thick darkness. The light failed to reach the back of the room, where the numerous control modules were located. He liked it that way, and it seemed appropriate for the occasion. And had it not been for the audio receivers, the darkness would've been matched only by the quiet.

Dr. Wallace Berente leaned forward. Tobacco smoke wafted between him and the screen. He drew a couple of times from his pipe, then held it in the monitor's light, as though to remind himself of a special detail. That detail was engraved on the stem as *R.B.* He stared at those initials intensely, as though they were staring back. Haunting him.

Dr. Berente's eyes return to the screen. The man he watched was a former intelligence officer named Steven Benelli. Berente, through various channels, had been keeping tabs on Benelli since he left the service. The man had gained ten pounds since returning to normal civilian life. Lack of stress probably allowed him to eat better. At age forty, he had served twenty years in the Central Intelligence Agency, of which thirteen were spent abroad in numerous countries that mostly would not be disclosed. But there was one country and date that Dr. Berente was well aware of. The only one that counted:

Haraz, Yemen – April 26th, 2016.

The memories played in his mind like archive footage. The dust deposits, the heavy cracks of gunfire, the intense heat that singed his

1

face. And worst of all, the sight of the tobacco pipe lying on the floor, smothered in blood. He stifled the memory of the body that lay beside it, and refocused on watching Steven Benelli on the screen. Benelli—the man who set his research back, was now the first live test subject for Dr. Berente's experiment.

The former agent slapped a few mosquitos that buzzed by his face as he walked through the jungle. He wandered between several thick trees, carefully looking over his shoulder every few steps. He gave up trying to reach out for any observers. Benelli wasn't stupid; he knew he'd been kidnapped. The only stupid part was not covering the tracks of his personal life. He had gotten comfortable in his civilian life and assumed his name was unknown to those he had investigated. Berente hadn't known initially. It took a little digging, but he figured out who was responsible for his setback, and his loss. He glanced at the initials again.

He heard a growl from a monitor to his left.

Dr. Berente looked over. The screen was dark. Not blank, there was just no light reaching the camera. He heard the movement though. The specimen was eager to be set free. It had been locked in its container for forty-eight hours now. Deliberately starved. It was getting angry and restless. He could hear its footsteps tapping the metal flooring.

Berente rolled his chair to the monitor and found the microphone linked to the speaker in its container. He leaned in, watching the darkness intently.

"I understand you're hungry. You have been very patient, all things considered." The sounds on the audio receiver ceased. The occupant had ceased its pacing. It was listening now. "This is an important lesson for you. You know what it's like to kill. But you don't know what it's like to hunt. From now on, if you wish to eat, you must hunt. Today will be your first lesson. There is food in the jungle. Fresh meat, full of blood to fill your stomach. You will feed. And once you've tasted the flesh, you will crave more."

The thing in the black listened to his hypnotic voice. After a minute of silence, he heard it growling again. It was ready.

"What the hell's going on? Why the hell was I dropped off in the middle of some jungle?"

Dr. Berente enjoyed listening to Benelli try to determine where he was. As he walked out of the frame, the computer switched to another nearby feed, tracking his movements as he went. Berente watched him studying the heights of the trees and the shapes of their leaves, as well as the climate surrounding it. It wasn't Florida. The topography was similar to that of Central American jungles, though he wasn't completely sure if that's where he was. He sniffed. There was salt in the air. The ocean was nearby.

Berente smiled as the former agent realized he was trapped on an island.

There were other things worrying the agent besides his location. He did not know the identity of his kidnappers. And there was the question of why they would go through all this trouble to capture him alive, and yet leave him unguarded and free to roam unsupervised.

The scientist was tempted to speak to him through an audio transmitter; to taunt him by letting him know who had captured him and why. The temptation faded after a brief moment. He ultimately didn't care about some grand scheme of letting his opponent know who defeated them, as though he was a villain in some spy novel. Berente's wish was simpler than that: he just wanted the pleasure of witnessing his revenge unfold. He wanted to see the author of his pain fall in a pool of his own blood and cry in agony.

The growling escalated into an enraged shriek. The specimen clawed at the walls, searching desperately for a way out. Berente returned to the microphone.

"Your time has come. Remember, you live because I breathed life into you. All I want in return is for you to give in to your instinct. This island is yours. Anything that walks on its soil is beneath you. Kill anything that dares to threaten your reign. I release you now, to hunt, to reign—to kill."

Between the monitors was a large control module, containing numerous instruments that enabled him to remotely control various devices across the entire island. He pulled up the controls for the *Site 5* elevator. He pressed a black button, raising the container from its underground location up to the earth's surface. An LED light blinked, indicating another control was on standby. Never taking his eyes off the screen, Berente pressed the button. He heard the sound of creaking metal. A bright light split down the center of the screen like blood seeping from a laceration. In an instant, the darkness had disappeared, and he saw jungle.

He watched his creature cover its eyes and adjust to the sunlight. Eager to feed, it stepped out and sniffed the air. Its prey wasn't far. It moved out of sight and disappeared into the forest.

Berente looked to the far wall, which displayed numerous monitors from all over the island. He isolated the northwest sector of the island where Site 5 was located. The monitors briefly went blank, then came back on again, only displaying the feed from that particular sector. His crew had worked tirelessly to place hidden cameras on the island. It was important to Berente that he didn't miss a thing.

He drew from his pipe and waited. He saw leaves rustling in one of the monitors, and the movement that caused it. His precious experiment moved like a ghost. Already, it was in tune with its surroundings. It was learning to adapt. There was an evolutionary instinct passed down from millions of years that couldn't be suppressed by any environment.

It moved like a ghost. Hardly a moment passed before he saw brief movement in another monitor. Its inner ears detected the faint echo from Benelli's footsteps. As it closed in, it detected vibrations caused by his movements. It was within a thousand feet of him now.

"I know you're out there!" Benelli shouted. The doctor smiled. Someone was out there, alright. Just not who he expected. The former agent shouted again, frustrated. *"You didn't bring me here for no reason! I don't presume you went through all this trouble just to bring me here to die! So, quit with your games."*

Dr. Berente smiled at the statements, specifically how wrong they were. The bastard didn't realize he was practically ringing the dinner bell. The doctor changed his mind: he would say something through the speaker. He got on the computer, pinpointed the precise location, and activated an audio transmitter located near the hidden camera.

"Foolish Agent Benelli." He watched as Benelli spun on his heel, searching for the source of his voice. "Twenty years in the agency should've taught you never to presume. Because, Agent Benelli, I did send you here to die."

The jungle exploded behind the agent, and a mass of teeth and claws descended upon him. The experiment moved at cheetah speed, impressive for its size and weight.

Dr. Berente drew on the pipe again. Grey smoke wafted between him and the screen, but it didn't dull the satisfaction of watching the fountain of blood burst from the agent's midsection. His screams turned to gargles. Chunks of flesh were torn free. Bones were smashed and limbs were pulled loose, all while the victim breathed his last. Berente watched the creature bite down on the agent's face, the ravenous teeth shredding his identity away in thin red ribbons.

A smile came over his face. The death was satisfying to watch. So much so, that he already craved more. He felt like a drug user that was instantly addicted with the first high. Luckily, plans were already in place. Agent Benelli was just the first piece of the puzzle. Soon, the other pieces would fall into place.

He sat and watched his creature ravage the corpse. It only took a few short minutes for it to expose the entire ribcage. It ate fast and enthusiastically. It had tasted human flesh now. As his master had told him, it would crave more.

CHAPTER 2

"Can I offer you bourbon? Coffee?" The man never looked up from the tablet provided by Dr. Berente.

Berente leaned back in the recliner, watching his sponsor's facial expressions as he watched the playback footage. There wasn't much audio other than that of Former Agent Benelli's attempt to trek through the island. The epic finale was yet to come.

"No, thank you," Berente replied. His tone was flat, his expression of noninterest in any of the features aboard the luxury yacht on which his sponsor had traveled on. This was business and nothing else.

A female assistant stepped in and provided coffee for the man.

"Please lower the blinds," he said to her, eyes never leaving the tablet. She walked to the window behind him and performed the request. A grey shadow swept over the maroon carpet and chair, erasing the sun's glare on the tablet screen.

Berente heard his own voice echo through the speakers, followed by screams and sounds of a struggle. The sponsor showed no disgust, rather, he nodded in satisfaction.

"I'm very impressed," he said. He watched for a few more seconds, then turned the tablet off. "*Very* impressed. Though, this could've been sent to me through video conference."

"I told you from the start," Berente said, "I conduct meetings in person. I'm not having my transmissions hacked by some computer nerd working for Interpol or the C.I.A. You show me an encrypted message and I'll show you someone who can crack it."

The sponsor leaned back.

"I have a list of buyers who are interested in your research. Terrorist organizations; governments; some acting as both. All are willing to pay top dollar and continue providing funding for this research. The dollar amount would be in the billions," he explained.

"I sense a 'but' on the end of that sentence," Dr. Berente said.

"They'll be very enthusiastic once I show them this footage. *But...* to really get the funds to support my business and your research, I'm gonna have to show them something real. A true demonstration."

Berente understood the underlying meaning. After all, an arms dealer like his sponsor wasn't in the process of selling pets. People interested in his genetic research were interested in the weapons capabilities of it. Berente anticipated his upcoming request. Not only that; he was counting on it.

"A demonstration, you say? You want a live-fire exercise," Berente confirmed. The sponsor nodded his head and took a sip of his expensive bourbon.

"Taking down an unarmed man is fun and entertaining to watch, but it won't mean much if the specimen is gunned down at first sight. These buyers want to see the tactical applications of the project. So, we need to throw this thing into the deep end—I want to see it go up against a squad of trained soldiers, armed with automatic weapons. If it is successful in eliminating the targets, then I guarantee these buyers will enthusiastically raise their bids. The funds will explode. You can create a hundred of these things, and make more off each one. Additionally, through them, I will be able to provide additional funding and test subjects. But first, we must provide them with a demonstration."

"That's no problem," Berente said. The Sponsor sat back.

"Excellent. I'll get right to work with my sources. Hiring someone to kill them is tricky business to say the least. Perhaps I can check with the private contractors I use to see if they have any—"

"I already have candidates for you," Dr. Berente interrupted him. He opened a small leather briefcase and retrieved a list of names and birthdates. The Sponsor took the paper and looked it over, then gazed back at Berente.

"These men—are you confident of their tactical efficiency?"

"Yes."

"Doctor," he spoke warningly, "you better be sure. My buyers can smell bullshit a mile away. And nothing will drive these people away faster than bullshit."

"I've seen them firsthand," Berente said. "Trust me. These people are the perfect test subjects for this exercise." The Sponsor looked over the names again.

"How do you know this information?" he asked.

"Let's just say I have a resource," Berente said. "But please feel free and conduct your own background checks."

"I will. I sense motive here," he said. "Something tells me these names are connected to the recent subject my contractors captured for you." Berente cocked his head to the side and shrugged his shoulders.

"They've never met," he said. "But they are connected. Think of them as different branches on the same tree."

The Sponsor crossed his arms and leaned forward. "And on the off-chance these people succeed, what are the odds they can trace all of this back to you?"

Berente grinned and shook his head.

"They don't even know I exist," he said. "They don't know me. But I know them. To me, this is more than a live-fire exercise. It's a ceremony, for both me, and him." He reached across the table and tapped his finger on the tablet, resuming the feed of his precious specimen gorging itself.

The sponsor watched, then looked again at the list.

"I'll see what I can do."

CHAPTER 3

"Focus on the front sight! Practice your fundamentals!" Rick Eilerman's voice boomed over the dozen police trainees. They were lined in a perfect row, spaced five feet from each other, listening to the orders of their firearms instructor. On his command, they drew their Glock 17s and aimed them at the paper targets twenty-five feet away.

Rick stepped to the side, keeping his eye on the nervous student at the end. The student turned his head slightly, noticing the forty-year old former marine standing there. Rick Eilerman had the presence of a Roman gladiator, and the physique of one too. Twenty-years in the U.S. Marine Corps, eighteen of those in Special Operations Command, was displayed in his appearance. Under that red trainer shirt were scars left from bullet and shrapnel wounds, one of which went from his bicep to his forearm. That visual history was enough for the cadet to know Rick did not have patience for nonsense.

"Eyes forward, Cadet. Focus on the suspect in front of you." Rick spoke softly but with severity. The cadet focused on the paper target with the human figure drawn printed with dotted lines. "Aim center mass. Be alert…and fire."

Several dozen cracks echoed through the summer air. Holes burst in the paper targets as most shots landed exactly where they were intended to go. It was a perfect day for this lesson. There was hardly a breeze or a cloud to distract the cadets. The only thing they had to endure was the heat and Rick's vigorous regimen. The sweat soaking through their training uniforms was not just from the ninety-five degree weather. Rick had them run several laps on the track, then jump hurdles, and climb a few walls. Now they had to concentrate and fight through their heavy breathing and aching muscles, while still aiming.

The cadets unloaded and placed their weapons on the tables in front of them. Rick proceeded to check the targets. He nodded with approval, seeing that most of the shots had found the center mass. There were a few misses, but it seemed each candidate had landed most of their rounds where they would inflict the most damage.

"Good. Well done. Third time's the charm," he said. He turned to face the group. "In a firefight, there's more to it than taking a stance, drawing a weapon, and squeezing the trigger. You'll have to endure the effects of dwindling stamina. Perhaps you've chased a suspect on foot for a mile or two, then he decides to take the situation to the next level and draw a weapon. Plus, there's the adrenaline you'll likely experience when the shit hits the fan. You need to understand how to react fast and efficiently, and to handle that tool properly when under duress. Understand?"

"Yes, sir," the group chanted.

"Good. Now hustle over to the box."

The 'box' was a twelve-by-twelve space with four portable barriers. The cadets formed a line outside, while an armorer waited at a table to provide tasers and simulation blank guns. Each one was loaded with a blue-coated blank round. Standing inside the box were two training assistants wearing full-body protective gear, which resembled black hazmat suits with plastic facemasks.

"Alright, boys and girls," Rick said. "You're going to take what you've learned and react to what you need to do. I don't want you to have time to think about it—it'll be a split-second reaction. This'll happen quickly, as most of what happens in law-enforcement and the military, happens very quickly. We're reactionary to whatever's in front of us. With reaction, you're behind the curve already. This drill is to build some tactics in your mind; that way you'll be able to act quickly in a scenario and have an advantage." He glanced at the cadet at the front of the line. Printed on his shirt was the name Baines. "Cadet Baines, you're first."

"Yes, sir," Baines replied. He stepped between the space between the walls, entering the box. Rick climbed a stepping ladder to allow him to observe the exercise from above.

"Face the wall," he told the cadet. Baines did as instructed, putting his nose to the blue tarp covering the barrier. Behind him, the two assistant trainers readied themselves to play the part of unruly suspects in a violent scenario. They gave a thumbs up to Rick, indicating they were ready. "Alright...ready, aaaaannd...action!"

Cadet Baines spun on his heel and saw the two 'suspects' engaging in a violent brawl. They threw punches at each other, then grappled, each attempting to strangle the other. Baines stepped forward and drew his taser.

"Break it up now!" he ordered in a firm voice. The two suspects broke it off and turned toward him. The one on the left approached with fists raised.

"You want some of this, cop?"

"I said STOP!" Barnes deployed the taser rods, planting them square in the 'suspect's' coat. He mimicked being electrocuted, then fell. He looked at the second one, who was also approaching in a similar manner. "Back up and lay on the ground, face first, arms out." The assailant kept coming.

"I'd run if I were you, cop! Don't have a taser now!" He started to close in. With the prongs latched in the downed suspect, Baines reached for his training Glock with his right hand, then aimed at the suspect.

"Last chance! Stop, or I will open fire," he said. The assailant backed away, fists lowered somewhat. "Get on the ground now!" Finally, the assailant lowered himself to the pavement and spread his arms and legs.

"Alright. Turn the taser off," Rick said. The Cadet did as instructed. "Turn around and face me. Okay. The situation is you had verbal noncompliance with the two suspects. They were confrontational, displaying acts of aggression toward you. One came in, arms raised, attempting psychological intimidation. You tasered him, took him down, the other came in. Same thing, aggressive behavior and psychological intimidation, while ignoring your warnings. Taser prongs were already lodged in the fallen suspect, leaving you one-handed and with no choice but to draw your Glock. You unholstered your weapon and warned him once more, to which he complied." Though speaking directly to Baines, he was loud enough to be heard by the whole class, intentionally giving them an idea of what they were doing in this drill, and eventually on the job. "Those actions are all within the department's policy. Well done," he completed.

Cadet Baines stepped out and Cadet Smith stepped in.

"Alright, Smith, are you ready?"

"Yes," he replied.

"We'll see. Face the wall." Cadet Smith did as instructed. A few moments passed as the assistants prepped the next scenario. After receiving the thumbs up, Rick yelled, "Action!"

Smith turned quickly and saw the two men in black suits. They were facing away from him, pressing a third person to the opposite wall. A holdup. Smith reached for his taser.

"Police! Get on the—" a gunshot rang out, and suddenly the victim fell flat on her back. Smith jolted, taken completely off guard. The men had pistols. He fumbled for his Glock, dropping the taser. The suspects turned and aimed their training pistols. Several more blanks rang out.

"Alright, you're dead," Rick said. Smith grimaced, embarrassed as he scooped up his taser and holstered it and his Glock. He faced the wall. His trainer glared down at him. "What the hell was that?"

Cadet Smith drew a breath. "There was a mugging. I thought the two men were unarmed."

"How would you have known that? You couldn't even see their hands. You went for your taser before you even understood the situation."

"It happened so fast. I thought—"

"That's the lesson, ladies and gents," Rick turned toward the other cadets. "There are times, whether in a traffic stop, a domestic violence call, or a drug raid…where you'll turn a corner and have to react instantaneously, while being aware of everything else that's going on around you."

Rick paused, seeing a flash memory of descending a stairwell in a dark brick building. Tremors shook the walls as explosions echoed from overhead. He descended into the bowels of the building, turned the corner and found the target. He squeezed the trigger and saw the pink mist.

Another explosion shook the building. He looked up and saw the ceiling tear open, and a wall of fire come down…

Rick snapped back into reality. He cleared his throat.

"Cadet Smith, get to the back of the line. Alright, who's next?"

The training continued until 7:00 that evening. Rick Eilerman was in his office, filling paperwork detailing the number of rounds spent and other supplies used. He could hear the cadets exiting the classroom down the hall to head home for the day. It seemed like a good group for the most part. They took his training seriously, even showing appreciation. Some of the other trainers had expressed the opinion that Rick's tactics courses were too advanced for new cadets—to which he told them where they could stuff that opinion.

These fucking instructors, two-thirds of them had never drawn a weapon in their entire lifetime. Good thing too, because had they been in such a situation, they probably wouldn't be alive right now. Yet, they were perfectly fine with providing mediocre training and sending young cops out into drug infested cities crawling with gang members who had no qualms about who they killed.

There was the reverberation of a buzzing phone in his desk drawer. It was the third time it had rung, not to mention the various text messages that had come in-between. Rick preferred to keep his phone tucked away when working, as to not get caught up in the rabbit hole of the internet.

He let out an exasperated sigh. He knew who was so eagerly trying to get in touch. A trace of guilt swirled in his stomach.

Best not to do it. You've already let this go too far. Finally, he dropped his pen and looked up, through the ceiling, at Heaven. He had no question of its existence; what he wasn't sure of was what his friend Danny was thinking. *Oh, buddy, you're probably hating my guts now.* How did angels think? Free from the mortal body, they were probably free of the judgement that haunted the human mind. At least, that's what Rick hoped. He never thought of the subject until recently.

Another text vibrated the desk. Rick gave in. He rushed a few notes on his sheet then finally checked his phone. There were four text messages and three missed calls from Ashley Rhee.

One simply read: *Hey.* Another: *Wanna get a bite to eat? We can have it here at my place.* The next was: *Hey. I was hoping to see you. Call me when you get off?* That damn question mark. Somehow, it added a level of sentimentality to the message. Rick felt the urge to type something back. "No." "Can't." "Sorry, I'm busy." Anything. Now the guilt was really eating at him.

Gosh, if Danny was here, he'd knock my fucking teeth out. He felt he'd deserve it too. Whoever wrote 'time heals all wounds' could go stick their head in a vice.

He'd known her as long as Danny had, which was a good ten years or more. He was best man at their wedding, and since Danny's funeral, he made a point to keep in constant contact with her. When he returned home on leave, he couldn't even look her in the eye. She always made him promise to bring Danny back to her. Not only did he fail to do so, he didn't even give her a body to bury.

His memory flashed to that crashing ceiling and enormous fireball. He remembered the hot burns he suffered to his left arm and shoulder and hot metal piercing his back. Most of all, he remembered how in one moment, Danny was right behind him, and in the next moment, he was gone, lost in three tons of burning debris. There was no reply to his name, no sign of him through the ruins. The rest of Fireteam Delta was outside, fending off advancing insurgents. There was no time: he had to leave his best friend for dead.

It had been four years, and both Ashley and Rick were still mourning Danny in their own ways. And three weeks ago, those ways came together, literally. It was just another routine get-together at her place with the other members of the old squad. It was a monthly thing, where all the guys met up at her place, barbequed and shared a few beers. It was their way of keeping Danny's memory alive. Rick was usually the last to leave, so it wasn't unusual to anyone that he remained behind when they took off. He'd usually hang around another twenty or thirty minutes, chitchatting and exchanging memories of the glory days with Ashley. Except, this time, their conversation lingered.

Pain followed the memories and a tearful Ashley found herself in the arms of an equally sorrowful Rick Eilerman. From there, everything else seemed to happen on their own. Their lips met, their bodies embraced, the clothing came loose. It seemed so automatic—including the guilt that followed. She asked him over the next night. He went, thinking she wanted to discuss what had happened, and figuring they would conclude that their passionate night would be a one-time thing. Instead, it became a two-night thing. Then three. Each time, the guilt worsened.

Rick felt numb as he stared at the phone until, finally, he began typing his response. "Sorry. Gotta work. Catch up another time, maybe." That sounded good. Simple and direct. Yet, he couldn't bring himself to hit *Send*. Somehow, blowing her off felt worse. Perhaps there was a middle ground. Maybe he would stop over, make sure she was doing okay, stay for some chit-chat and a beer, then leave. Just like old times. He deleted the message and replaced it with "Leaving work now. I'll stop over for a min."

He stood up, switched off the light, and locked the door behind him on his way out.

CHAPTER 4

The sun was slowly beginning its descent behind the horizon, its gold evening rays blinding as Rick took a left turn. He squinted, barely able to make out the traffic light signals in the upcoming intersections. After the third one, he entered a suburban community with lots of trees which spared his eyes from the strain. He took a right and continued until he came to a lilac grey house with a white Chevy in the driveway. Four years ago, there was a Dodge Ram next to it. It was almost brand new, and since it had no driver and she had to cut corners to save money and keep the house, Ashley had to sell it.

Rick parked alongside the Chevy then approached the door. It opened right as he started reaching for the handle, revealing a golden-skin woman with long sparkling amber hair.

"Hi," Ashley Rhee said, smiling.

"Hey," Rick said. She let him in. He stopped briefly, debating whether or not to take his boots off. Doing so would imply he intended to stay a while, but the hardwood floor still looked as new as when Danny and Ashley bought the place. Out of respect, he slipped them off and placed them on the mat near the door. The living room and kitchen was one big room, separated by a bar counter. On it was an open bottle of wine and two glasses. Rick inhaled. He didn't want to look at her now, not dressed in that loose blue tank and short jean shorts. He could see from the low neckline and shoulder straps that she wasn't wearing a bra underneath.

He cleared his throat. "How's the classes going?" *Or was it one summer class she was teaching?* It wasn't often Rick's usually focused mind was in a loop.

"It got cancelled, actually," she said. "Too many kids dropped out. Couldn't handle the five hour course, much less the accelerated assignments and tests. Got the call today that there were less than ten remaining, so they cancelled it."

"Who wants to spend their summer writing essays, anyway?" Rick said.

"Or grading papers," Ashley added, smiling. She was relieved, which somewhat surprised Rick.

"You volunteered for that," he said. "Don't you need the money?"

"I'm doing fine," she answered. She went for the counter and started pouring wine into both glasses. "I'd rather have the summer. Besides, the truck's almost paid off. I don't have any other debt except for the house, so…" she shrugged her shoulders then handed a glass to Rick. His lips barely touched the glass when he noticed her move closer. His eyes couldn't help but go to that neckline. They traveled the edge of that tank top, inviting him to see the soft flesh beneath. The straps were practically on the verge of falling off her shoulders.

He looked away, as though drawn by some magical force to the living room bookshelf. Up on the top was Danny's picture, after his promotion to Corporal. The frozen image seemed to stare Rick in the eyes, piercing his soul.

Dude, I never looked at her this way before, I swear. Not until three weeks ago. And even then, I never thought of her as...it just happened. It was spontaneous. Just emotional and physical instinct acting together. Gosh, the guy had been dead for four years, but it didn't matter. It still felt like he was cheating with his wife.

"Have we made a date for the next get-together?" he asked.

"Angelo's out of the county at the moment," Ashley said. "I shot him a text a couple of days back. Not sure what the others are up to." By the way she spoke, it was clear she wasn't interested in talking about the guys. "You've hardly touched your wine."

Rick looked at his glass then back at her. Her glass was empty and back on the countertop. Rick smiled then sipped again. Ashley approached, coming right into his space. He could feel her grazing her finger around the waistline of his jeans. That graze turned into a light pinch, and she gently began untucking his shirt. He felt the rush of feelings that led to their last encounters. Already, he was growing weak. His conscious mind barked orders at him, reminding him of the guilt he would feel afterwards.

"I…uh," Rick pulled back gently. Ashley stood still for a moment with a hint of disappointment on her face, which she immediately tried to conceal by looking neutral. "Sorry." Rick put the glass down. "It's not you, it's just..."

"Damn right it better not be me," she chuckled. The sassiness in her voice was much appreciated. Rick chuckled.

"Girl, you have nothing to worry about in that regard. I used to ask Danny how a skinny little Asian like him managed to score someone like you." Ashley smiled at the thought. She looked at the picture, then back at Rick.

"You don't need to feel bad," she said. "What happened, happened. And...I'm not sorry."

"Thank you for saying that," Rick said. "I guess I feel like I've somehow gone behind his back. Maybe I feel like he's still alive somehow..." *Goddamn, keep your thoughts to yourself.* He thought of the collapsing building, not seeing Danny. Hell, he wasn't sure if the guy was dead. The internal guilt assault began, along with the rationalization. *He couldn't have survived it. And you had the rest of your team to save.*

"I...I guess I should go," he said.

"You don't have to," Ashley said. "We can sit and talk." She took a seat on the couch, as though to demonstrate. Rick felt the pull to join her. It won. He sat beside her and leaned back. He felt the cushion with his hands. Memory foam.

"When did you get this?" he asked.

"Had it delivered Monday," she replied. Rick let himself sink into it. It was so comfortable, he almost forgot his struggle. He noticed a second couch across from where they sat, along with a chair, all made from the same material. *Where the hell did she get the money for all this furniture?* He decided not to ask. What difference did it make anyway?

"I know I had you promise a hundred times to bring him back," Ashley said, "but, even when you didn't, I never begrudged you. It's time you move on."

He looked over at her.

"Have you moved on?"

She ran a hand onto his shoulder, the fingertips slipping under the sleeve.

"I have to," she said. "I can't go on being in pain forever. I don't want to spend each night fixating on it. I'm by myself all the time, and I'm not supposed to be. It's not fair and..." emotion was streaming from her voice now. She leaned forward and buried her head in his arms. They hugged tight, pressing their heads together.

His hands felt the skin on her back. Passion caused intense breathing. Ashley pressed her lips to his. Rick didn't resist. His guard was down; he was giving in again. Tongues entwined and hands grabbed at each other's bodies. Rick wrapped his muscular arms under her butt, lifted her off the couch and carried her into the bedroom.

Her tank top came off with little effort, exposing her plum breasts. After removing his shirt, Ashley grabbed him by the back of his head and lowered him to her chest as though demanding he run his lips along her skin. As he did, she undid his belt buckle, then slipped out her shorts, offering her naked body to Rick. With a tug on his jeans, he was equally bare. Breathing and moaning, Ashley dug her tongue into his mouth, pulling him into position. Rick felt her ankles lock behind his back, trapping him. She wanted him here, and nowhere else. Desperately.

He entered her, thrusting slowly. Ashley responded with a pleasured moan, tilting her head back to keep Rick nipping at her neck and shoulders. She clawed at his back, spurring him on. His pace gradually intensified. It was like electricity was coursing through their bodies. Heavy breathing filled the room, and like two simultaneous explosions, they climaxed together.

They remained entangled in each other's arms, neither saying a word. There was no telling how much time had passed before Rick finally started pulling away. He leaned up no more than a few inches before Ashley locked her hand on the back of his neck, rolled him over and straddled him.

"You're not going anywhere," she insisted, smiling. She began her attack, kissing and nipping at his neck. She proceeded to work him up for another round of passionate lovemaking, which would continue long into the night.

CHAPTER 5

The lovemakers carried on long into the night, until finally they both passed out into a deep sleep. Rick didn't even have time to feel guilty; the sleep hit that quick. Everything simply went to a series of dreams that only made sense to the unconscious mind. But no matter how deeply he slept, there was always a part of Rick's brain that was on alert. He had spent years in Iraq, Yemen, Afghanistan, Nigeria, as well as a few locations he wasn't allowed to mention. Often, he and his squad would have to find a place to hunker down and rest. When in enemy territory, with no extraction, he learned to sleep with one eye open. He taught himself to respond to the faintest sounds—often, the faintest sounds were the most troubling. It meant someone could be approaching, trying hard not to be seen or heard. It was one of many things that stuck with him after leaving the service.

Rick thought it was his imagination when he awoke. It sounded like footsteps. Slow footsteps, like what he'd make when approaching an enemy camp. Was it his imagination? Possibly; he'd awakened in the middle of the night before, thinking someone was right outside his house, only to realize it was the neighbor getting home late. Still...

He pulled on his pants and moved to the corner of the window. He saw the lawn. No movement. For several moments, there was other silence. He looked back to the bed. Ashley was still asleep, facing away from him.

Gosh, I must be going crazy...

Something shifted on the other side of the house. The sound was faint. Alarm bells went off in his mind. There was another faint sound. Fabric on a hard ledge. Feet on a countertop. Barely audible. The untrained ear wouldn't have picked up on it.

19

Barefoot and bare-chested, Rick moved into the hallway. Nobody in the kitchen or living room. Further back in the house was another small hallway going into the spare room, bathroom, and utility room. He hurried to the edge of the hall, standing just out of view, listening for the sound of a door handle. There wasn't one, but he did hear soft footsteps. The laundry room door was probably already open.

There was definitely someone in the hallway.

Next was a voice so low, it was barely a whisper.

"Bedroom's in there. Go. Go. Go."

Only six words, but they weren't spoken like common thugs. Rick felt the vibe of a professional. That, and most everyday thugs wouldn't have soundlessly made their way in.

Shit!

Rick felt anger and a sense of powerlessness. Had this happened at home, he'd have a whole assortment of weapons to fight them off. In fact, they'd even have a hard time getting in without triggering one of his alarm systems. Neighbors thought him to be paranoid. *If only they were here to see this.*

He remembered his training, and recognized a mistake in his thoughts—he *did* have one weapon in his arsenal: himself.

They approached the edge of the hall. There was just enough light to allow Rick to see the muzzle of a handgun. The man holding it was dressed head-to-toe in black tactical gear including a facemask. There was one other behind him, carrying a rifle of some sort. By the time they saw Rick, he had already sprung.

He threw a kick, knocking the one with the rifle backwards, then grabbed the first one by the wrist. He struck the intruder with an elbow to the nose, splashing blood, then twisted his wrist back until the pistol was dislodged. Using his bodyweight, he rammed the enemy shoulder-first into the corner, breaking his collarbone. The other thug rose to his knees and pointed his rifle. Rick turned, dragging the injured prowler in his path. The human shield jolted as he absorbed the projectile. Rick tossed his limp body to the side and leapt onto the other, driving him back onto the floor.

Rick knocked the weapon free and drove an elbow into his throat. Gasping for breath, the prowler still tried to overpower the marine, but failed miserably and was rolled over on his stomach and placed in a chokehold. There were more footsteps, now coming from other parts of the house.

Who the hell are these guys? How many of them are there?

Rick tightened the chokehold until the combatant finally went limp, then immediately went for his sidearm. A Sig Saur P226, .40 caliber, with a suppressor. The living room window opened. Rick went to the corner and took aim. The men coming through were also dressed in tactical gear. The first was shocked to see a gun pointing at him. His hesitation cost him his life. The pistol shots, though suppressed, still let off an audible crack. The intruder absorbed the rounds in the chest and fell back.

He continued firing, driving off the others that were about to follow. He heard glass shattering somewhere to his right. The spare bedroom. He turned, saw the armed man stepping out, rifle aimed. Rick fired first. The man was hit in the shoulder, jolting him to the left, and throwing off his aim. The projectile hit the wall near Rick's head. It stuck from the plaster, like a mosquito on a horse. For a brief instant, it drew Rick's eye. A tranquilizer dart. He fired another round, finishing off the perp. The slide locked back.

"Shit."

Another man was stepping out. Rick sprinted, sneering, hands open. He was too late. Before he even heard the crack of the pistol, he felt the sting of the dart in his chest. Its effect was instantaneous. But Rick was committed to the attack, driven by adrenaline and sheer will. He drove the gunman to the wall. Already, Rick was losing balance. His arm raked across the gunman's face, ripping the mask away, revealing the man underneath. His skin was scaly, as though dragged through acres of road. Scars lined the forehead below the widow's peak lined with short, blond hair. Rick rammed an elbow into his eye, followed with a left hook to the chin. The assailant took the blow, nearly went down, but held his balance. Bracing against the wall, he threw a kick into Rick's chest, knocking him back.

Rick was feeling wobbly. He fought against the drug, but determination had little power over its effect. His vision blurred. With the room dark to begin with, he was practically blind. The man closed the distance and hit him with an uppercut to the chin. Rick hit the ground. He rolled to get to his knees, but his body gave up halfway through. He thought of Ashley. What would they do with her? That thought plagued his dreams as he faded into unconsciousness.

The gunman took in a deep breath, then stood over his target.

"The boss wasn't kidding. The fucking guy's tough." His men flooded the house and secured all the rooms.

"Crap," one of them said, seeing his dead companions, then back at his leader. "Damn it, Kruse. We were told this would be a simple op."

"Nothing's ever simple," Kruse said.

"He saw your face," another said.

"It doesn't matter. Let's stop wasting time. Get the girl. Take him to the chopper. Take the bodies out, and get a crew to fix the window. Don't leave any trace."

CHAPTER 6

When Rick woke up, he was on his back, laying on a hard surface with no padding. Through blurry vision, he stared up at a steel ceiling that was barely visible in the dim light. His fingertips grazed the floor around him. It was metal too.

Memories of recent events flashed in his mind like strobing lights, sparking a rush of adrenaline. He sat up quickly and raised a fist, ready to take on anyone in the room. His eyes panned around the dark enclosure, seeing windowless walls. He was alone. He was still shirtless, wearing only the jeans that he wore when he was abducted.

He thought of the armed men, invading the house…

"Oh, God…Ashley."

He looked around again, but without windows, he had no way of figuring out where he was. The enclosure was fifteen feet long, roughly eight feet wide. All metal. Whoever these people were, they had dropped him off inside of a small shipping container.

On the far end to his left, he could see latches fastened in thick slots. A door. He closed the distance in a few strides.

"Hey!" he shouted. There was no response. He banged on the door. "Hey. Open up. Where the hell am I?" Several more minutes of banging and shouting followed. It was clear that either there was nobody on the other side, or if there was someone there, they were extremely patient. Either way, he wasn't getting a response.

With nothing else to do, Rick turned around and continued examining the room. At the back of the container, a small battery-powered lantern hung from a hook in the ceiling. Below it was a few bottles of water, some protein bars, and a pile of clothes with a note reading, *"Put these on. You'll need them."*

Rick knelt down to examine the clothes. There was a black t-shirt, black tactical pants, combat boots, socks, a duty belt with an empty thigh holster, and a tactical vest. He checked the sizes and was surprised to see that everything was measured to his size. Either they checked him, or they somehow already knew.

He was wary of putting them on; anything these bastards wanted him to do, he didn't trust. Then again, if they wanted him dead, he'd be dead. He checked the vest. There was nothing in the pockets. His eyes went to the empty holster.

What the hell's going on? If they're making me wear this, does that mean they're gonna give me weapons?

That didn't make sense. Why arm someone you kidnapped in the middle of the night? His mind ran through a dozen possibilities. Forced assassination seemed plausible, especially if they were using Ashley as leverage.

"Christ, I might as well be in a goddamn Schwarzenegger movie, if that's the case," he said to himself. He picked up the shirt. *Better than being half naked, I suppose.*

He changed into the clothing, fastened the belt around his waist, and slipped into the vest. It had been a while since he had worn one, even longer since wearing an empty one. He didn't like the weight, or lack thereof.

Minutes passed. Rick paced around the walls, searching for any holes or cracks, but found none. He completed several passes, then found himself staring at the door, tempted to knock again. Being a man of common sense, he knew better than to waste his energy. He grabbed his jeans, wadded them into a ball, and used them as a seat cushion.

He cracked open a water bottle, took a sip, and waited. It was all he could do.

CHAPTER 7

The next forty minutes passed in silence. Sipping water and staring at the wall across from him, he was able to pick up on little details. There were faint vibrations underneath him, which he believed were from large engines. In addition, there was a slight, hardly noticeable, swaying sensation. At first, he thought it was an after-effect of the tranquilizer. But he had been on ships enough times in his life to know he was on one.

Why was he on a ship, and where was he going? If anywhere?

The silence was abruptly broken by a pounding on the other side of the door. Rick jumped to his feet, hands raised in a combative pose. The latch retracted with a sharp whine, then opened a crack. Blinding light seeped through. Light—it was daytime, at least he knew that much. Surprisingly, it stung Rick's eyes more than he expected. Still, he kept them on the crack in the door. The space was just wide enough for Rick to see that the figure on the other side had an MP5 pointed right at him. No tranquilizers this time.

"Move to the back of the wall," the man ordered.

"Where's Ashley?" Rick said.

"You want her to stay in one piece, you'll do as I say."

The bastard knew what to say. Rick clenched his jaw, raised his hands over his shoulders, and slowly backed up until he was pressed against the far side. The guards widened the door. There were three of them, all dressed in the same tactical gear as those who invaded Ashley's house. A fourth one stepped into view, unarmed, and by the look of the way he walked, off balance. His vest and holster were empty. It was obvious to Rick that this individual had been kidnapped in the dead of night as well, then forced into wearing this gear. One of the armed guards struck him in the stomach, doubling him over, then with the aid of another guard, threw him into the container.

The door slammed shut and latched again.

The man on the floor rolled to his side and looked back. "I've seen Coast Guard cadets that could hit harder than you!"

"Seems to have done the job," Rick said. He approached the man and held out a hand to help him up. As he pulled him to his feet, the lantern's dim rays came onto his thin black hair and hooked nose. Both men's eyes widened. "Ranch?!"

"Rick-fucking-Eilerman!"

The two men briefly embraced in a hug.

"Damn, you'd think I'd've picked up on that annoying Tennessean accent of yours," Rick said.

"Well, you must really be off your game if these guys got you," Ranch said. He started walking around the container, examining the walls.

"Don't bother, I've already looked. There's no way out," Rick said. Ranch groaned, then crossed his arms. He had a similar build as Rick, maybe slightly skinnier. His head was showing the early signs of balding, which started in their last months of service. Normally, Rick would seize the opportunity to poke fun at him for it, but considering the situation, neither of them were in a mood to kid around.

Ranch looked down at the protein bars and water.

"Well, they don't want us dead," he said.

"As of right now, at least," Rick said. Ranch shook his head slightly, turned, then kicked the wall in frustration. He paced for a few more moments, then slumped to the floor.

"What the hell's going on?" he said. "You have any fucking idea who these people are?"

"Not a clue," Rick answered. He was content to stay standing. "Did they tranq you?"

Ranch looked up at him and nodded. "Yeah."

"What's the last thing you remember?" Rick asked.

"Waking up in a helicopter," Ranch answered. "A refinished Stallion. Whoever these guys are, they've got funds. And enough arsenal to supply a small army."

"And before that?"

"Before that, I was home on Ayres Avenue. I woke up for a sec, just in time to see these guys come into my bedroom with guns. Next thing I knew, I was out." He leaned over for a bottle of water. He examined the lid, then squeezed it hard, seeing if any needle holes had been poked into it. *Not drinking any drugs these guys slipped into this bottle.* Rick knew what he was doing.

"If they wanted to drug us, they'd have stuck us with whatever they wanted on the flight here," he said. It was a fair point. Still, Ranch smelled the water, then took a taste. Nothing he could detect. Plus, it was clear Rick had been drinking his and was showing no adverse effects. "Speaking of here…" Rick continued, "where is here?"

"I don't know," Ranch said. "All I can say is that it's in the middle of the ocean."

"No land?"

"Negative. No land in sight. Without a satellite, there's no way we can figure out on our own where the hell we are." He took a swallow. "You know? I'm surprised they managed to get ahold of you, Mr. Prepper. Hell, whenever I come to visit you, I'm afraid I'll step on a damn land mine."

"I wasn't home," Rick answered. "I was, uh, visiting Ashley. Didn't have my guns on me. Nor my alarm system. Bastards are holding her hostage, but I don't know where."

"You've been visiting her frequently," Ranch said. He glanced over at the jeans. "No shirt. No shoes!" He looked back up at Rick. A smirk formed over his jawline. Rick shook his head.

"I was there to, uh—"

"Relax, man," Ranch chuckled. "You guys have gotten close. I get it." He stood back up. Floor was getting uncomfortable anyway. "*Danny* would be okay with it. Don't beat yourself up."

"I will if these jackasses do anything to her," Rick said, looking back at the door.

"Depends on what they want *us* to do," Ranch said, looking down at his vest. "Any clues."

"Just guesses," Rick said. "Maybe they want us for target practice. Another thought was they wanted to frame us for some political crime. With Ashley being held hostage—" He cringed, hating even acknowledging that fact, "I've thought perhaps they wanted to force us to do a job of some kind."

"In that case, they should've just sent the guys they hired to kidnap us. They seem pretty good," Ranch said. "Or hire Adkin and his group."

"How's he doing?"

"Spoke to him not long ago. He seems to be doing pretty good. I'm starting to wish I joined up with him."

"You're no mercenary. Atkin was a good marine, but he took a little *too* much glee in killing," Rick said, his voice showing disdain. *Then again, I'm probably not one to talk. Right now, I'd personally take great pleasure in snapping the neck of every one of these bastards.* He briefly thought of his old unit, Fireteam Delta, wishing they were here to back him and Ranch up and get them out of this mess. A thought crept into his mind. "Does it not seem odd that they've specifically targeted you and me? Members of the same fireteam?"

Ranch thought about it. "It would be an odd coincidence if unintended."

"When was the last time you heard from the others?" Rick asked.

"Not since our last get-together at Ashley's," Ranch said. "I know Bellville stated he was going up to his cabin for the weekend. If these guys know where we live, then hopefully he got up there. Last night was a Friday night, so Shaw and Healy were probably making their rounds at the strip joint on Cassidy Drive. Knowing fucking Shaw, he was probably banging one or two of the strippers afterward. Hopefully he was, and at her place."

"Not sure if that would've helped," Rick said. "They tracked me down to Ashley's."

"For these guys to be this precise, they'd have to have been studying our movements and habits for a while. Hell, they probably hacked your phone and used it to trace your location. You leave it in that desk of yours at work. Anyone with half a brain can pick a lock."

Rick nodded. It was possible. And they couldn't be sure if the rest of the team was being tracked down, or if it was just he and Ranch.

"If we're on the ocean, then there's no calling 9-1-1," he muttered.

"Or an airstrike," Ranch said. He kicked the wall again, though not as hard this time. He started to pace anxiously. He hated confined spaces. The stale smell of rusted metal didn't help. He walked along the wall, then slumped against the corner.

"I suppose you've already tried communicating with them," he said.

Rick nodded. "Yeah. No luck. It's clear they have no intention of speaking with us at the moment. As you've pointed out, if they wanted us dead, we'd be dead. They're using us for something."

"Yeah, but what?" Ranch said. "And why out here in the middle of the ocean?"

"I don't know. But when they're ready, they'll let us know."

Ranch sighed and threw up his hands in displeasure. "I guess we just wait." It was the worst part of combat: not the drills; not the patrols, not even the firefights. It was the damn waiting that every marine hated. Only this time, they had to do it in a tin box, with no idea what laid ahead. Ranch groaned. "Fuck these assholes!"

CHAPTER 8

Rick Eilerman leaned against the wall, counting down the seconds while staring at the dull steel across from him. He predicted that an hour had passed since Ranch arrived. His companion was lying on the floor, tossing bottle caps at the wall. The boredom only added to the anxiety and anticipation he felt. There hadn't been a single sound from outside since the guards put him in the container, except for wind and ocean waves.

Ranch was back on his feet and starting his hundredth round of nervous pacing.

"I swear I'm gonna put my fist through that door," he said.

"You'll break your hand," Rick said.

"I know. I'm just venting," Ranch replied. "I forgot, you never had a sense of humor unless you were stateside."

"It's called focus," Rick said.

"I guess I've lost my touch," Ranch said. He kicked the door, then noticed Rick shake his head and look away. "Oh? You don't approve?"

"You're wasting energy," Rick said.

"You know me. I'm not good with tight spaces. Hence I chose the marines over prison." Ranch leaned against the wall and briefly thought of his past. Good thing the military wasn't as strict on their recruits having squeaky clean backgrounds back then as they are today. His arrest for hotwiring a corvette and driving off with it would certainly have left a red mark on his record. *Ah, the good ol' days of rebellious youth.*

He sighed, then started going through the catalog of missions in his mind.

"What about Bosnia? Those Bosniak guys? I know we pissed a lot of them off when we went over there. That was my first deployment in '97."

"Unless someone in the C.I.A. gave up our names, I doubt it," Rick said. "And why wait this long to do it?"

"That's a fair point." Ranch was quiet for a moment. He turned around and stared at the wall. It wasn't the structure that had his attention. He knelt down, trying to feel any vibrations from the deck. He looked up at Rick. "Is this ship moving?"

Rick felt the floor.

"I don't think so," he replied. "Don't have much to go on. It's hard to tell from in here."

"It was moving before," Ranch said. "I think we've stopped." Rick pressed his ear to the wall and listened.

"I think I hear footsteps," he said. Ranch did the same. For a few moments, he didn't hear anything. Then there it was: boots tapping on a metal deck. There were voices, speaking just low enough to be heard. He moved to the center of the container and faced the door, hands poised to grab anyone on the other side.

"No," Rick whispered. Ranch glared at him, a silent rebellion. "Marine, we're outmatched. They'll gun us down if they have to. They're keeping us alive for a reason. Let's figure out what it is."

Ranch didn't hear Rick Eilerman the civilian—he heard the voice of his Fireteam Sergeant in the USMC. He straightened his posture and backed from the door.

"Can't blame me for wanting a good fight," he said. Rick ran his thumb over his empty holster.

"Something tells me we're in for one, whether we want to or not."

The two men waited and listened. After a while, the people outside did nothing to hide their presence. They spoke loud and sternly, directing somebody. There were mild sounds of a struggle, followed by some cursing. It was clear there were more prisoners aboard this ship.

A guard knocked on the door. "Put your backs to a wall and keep clear of the door!"

Rick backed up first. Ranch hesitated, still tempted to ambush and fight, but it took only a little common sense to know he'd be riddled with holes and left to bleed out on the floor. He backed up next to Rick, then looked over at him.

"You think they're putting more people in?"

"They don't need to stop the boat for that," Rick said. "Not if they were delivered by chopper."

"I didn't hear chopper blades," Ranch said. Rick watched the door as the guards turned the latch. It was true; he would've certainly heard any aircraft.

The door opened, letting in a stream of blinding light. The guards peered inside, saw that the prisoners had complied, then opened it the rest of the way. He and two other guards, all armed with MP5 submachine guns, entered the container and pointed their muzzles at the two men.

"Step outside. *Slowly*," the middle one said. With their hands raised behind their heads, Rick and Ranch walked for the door. Two other guards waited on the right side. The prisoners winced as they stepped into the hot sunlight. A light breeze swept across their faces.

"Eilerman? Ranch?"

Rick's vision cleared up, and right away he spotted Belville's hulking physique and square jaw.

"Jesus, they've got you too?" Ranch said.

"I had no chance. These assholes were waiting for me, right there in the driveway of my cabin. Thought it was the damn I.R.S. for a moment, until the damn tranq dart hit me."

"Jesus," Rick said. He looked at Ranch. "We were right. They've been tracking us."

"Anyone else with you?" Ranch asked.

"Shaw and Healy," Bellville replied. "They had us in a container back there. Shaw, uh, they're bringing him. He tried to disarm one of them when they opened our container. Took the butt of a rifle to the back of the head, so he's a little hazy. Healy's with him. He's a better medic than any of these pricks have to offer."

Rick glanced at Belville's vest, holster, and pants. They'd matched everything to his size, even the boots for his surprisingly average-sized feet. He glanced back. The guards were standing in a single row, watching them, but not making any effort to stop them from conversing.

"I don't suppose you have any clue what they want?" he said.

"They didn't tell me a thing," Belville said. "Just gave me this stuff and made me change into it."

"What's this place?" Ranch asked, pointing into the ocean. Nearly a mile off the starboard bow was a small island. From what they could see, it couldn't be any more than a couple of miles wide. There was a high canopy. No clear view of a landing site, but then again, it was hard to tell from this far out.

"I have no idea what this place is, or *where* it is," Belville replied. "But I don't think it's a coincidence that we've stopped here."

31

"Great. So, their plan is to cast the *Gilligan's Island* reboot," Ranch said. He looked back at the guards, none of whom offered a response. They simply stared, eyes cold, void of humanity, their guns pointed to the deck. "I guess not."

Rick looked up at the sun. Judging by its position, the time was between 10:00 and 11:00 in the morning. The sky was clear. The ocean was calm. There was no obvious indication of previous conflict in the area.

He stepped close to the portside railing for a better look at the island. At that moment, he noticed a seaplane taking to the air. Judging by its trajectory, it had landed in the water on, judging by the position of the sun, the northeast side of the island.

"Supply plane?" Ranch asked.

"Maybe they're dropping someone else off," Belville said.

"Or both," Rick added.

They turned around, hearing footsteps from around one of the other containers. They heard someone stumble, and others rushing.

"Come on, pick up the pace," a guard said.

"He's fine, I got him."

Rick recognized Healy's voice, as well as his wrinkly face, aged from years of stressful combat conditions. Stumbling alongside him was Shaw. The youngest of the group, the bald thirty-two year old was built like an action figure, his body lean and muscular. The back of his head was red from being struck with a rifle. His senses were still coming back to him. It took Healy's mention of Rick's name for him to realize the rest of Fireteam Delta was standing here on the deck with them.

"Holy Shit, Sarge. I thought it was just us," he said.

"If only I could be that lucky," Rick said. He tapped Healy on the shoulders, then turned to Shaw. "You alright, kid?"

"Just got a little too excited, boss," Shaw said. "Had 'em on the ropes though."

"I'm sure you did," Rick replied. He then lowered his voice and leaned in toward Healy, "Any of you guys hear from Adkin? Did they get him too?"

"No," Healy said.

"It's no coincidence they've nabbed all of us," Belville said. "Perhaps this is the government's work."

"Nah, they'd just pick active duty marines," Rick said. "Much less effort, and could easily be written off as a training exercise. Whoever's running this, they have an agenda."

"And who's the *who*?" Ranch said.

"Not your concern," a thundering voice boomed from behind the next container. All eyes turned to the large, scabby faced leader of the mercenaries. Rick instantly recognized him from the previous night. As the tranquilizer took its effect, he had heard one of the other men call him by name.

What was it? Began with a K. Kreese? King? Krom...KRUSE!

"Kruse," he said aloud. The mercenary's eyes widened briefly, then returned to their dark, emotionless state. Who cared if these guys knew his name?

Kruse snapped his fingers at the row of mercenaries.

"Bring 'em."

The guards circled behind the prisoners, goading them with their weapons. Shaw flinched, resisting the temptation to try and disarm them, then walked with the others sternward.

"So, what is this? What's the big idea, bringing us out into the middle of nowhere?" Ranch said.

"Why are you making us wear this gear?" Belville added.

"I'm starting to feel like I'm reenacting *The Most Dangerous Game*," Healy said. Without answering, Kruse continued to lead them to the structure. A crane hovered overhead, its harness strung to a twelve-foot Zodiac inflatable.

"Get inside," he said.

"Not until you tell us what's going on," Shaw growled. MP5 muzzles pointed at them, their handlers growing uneasy. Kruse, on the other hand, maintained his calm, expressionless demeanor.

"You will take this boat to the northwest shore," he said. "There you will find supplies and instructions. There will be other members of your party waiting there. Don't be alarmed when you see them. They've been notified of your arrival."

"If we refuse?" Rick asked.

"Then I'll stop wasting time and just have my men unload on all of you, right here and now," Kruse answered. "It's your choice. All I can tell you is, if you want to live, you're better off following our instructions." He reached into his pocket and pulled out a square-folded piece of paper, then extended it to Rick. "This is a map of the island. It'll help you keep track of where you are. The 'X' is the landing site where your supplies are located. It'll be more than enough for your test."

"*Test?*" Rick asked.

"You'll understand when you get there," Kruse said.

"Who are these other guys in our 'party'?" Healy asked.

"No more questions," Kruse said, his voice containing a hint of hostility. "Get in the boat. Now. The fun is only just beginning."

The men looked at each other. They shared the same bad gut feeling. Suddenly, that little green island didn't look so tranquil anymore. There was an evil beyond those rocky shores, and they were being fed right to it.

Unfortunately, that island was the only place where they had a fighting chance.

"Get in," Rick said. His voice was calm and collected, much like it was in their numerous tours in the Middle East. As though on active duty, the prisoners followed the command of their Sergeant and entered the Zodiac. Rick took a seat in the front next to Ranch. He recognized the look on the former Force Reconnaissance specialist's face.

I hope you know what you're doing.

Rick leaned a few millimeters toward him and cocked his head toward the island. Ranch understood the unspoken message.

I don't. But we're dead either way.

The mercenaries lowered the boat into the water.

"Enjoy yourselves," Kruse shouted to them. His voice lacked the to-the-point emotionless tone, and now sounded like that of a giddy twelve year old holding a magnifying glass over a colony of ants in the hot sun. Shaw, Healy, and Ranch raised their middle finger at him.

"Focus, guys," Rick said. The boat touched down into the water. Belville undid the cables and started the motor. It came on with a dull, sputtering sound, then pushed the boat forward. Belville turned the lever, steering the group toward the mysterious island.

CHAPTER 9

The closer view of the island brought forth greater detail of its landscape. The entire west shore was lined with jagged rocks, which provided no safe place to land. Two miles south was an elevation, which ultimately led to a huge cliff-shelf that overlooked the Pacific. It was so large, it could be spotted with the naked eye as they approached the northwest corner. As they got close, Rick's eyes moved from the cliffs to the northeast peninsula on his left. This island couldn't have been any larger than four miles in diameter.

Wild birds flew overhead. Waved albatrosses with black bodies, white necks, and yellow beaks circled high above the west shore. A harpy eagle descended to the northeast, seemingly making a dive straight into the earth. When it seemed it would plummet, it angled back to the skies, now with a large snake caught in its talons.

The island's interior was jampacked with breadnut trees, Rhamnaceae trees, low-leaning Calophyllum trees, and many others that couldn't be distinguished from afar. However, it was enough for Rick to know that this island was relatively untouched by any government or major business entity for that matter. If someone did own it, and he suspected they did, they either didn't have the resources to clear it out, or simply didn't want to. And it was clear that the people who kidnapped Rick and his former team had the financial resources to clear out some space. Perhaps they had something on the other side of the island, but so far, this speck of green on the map looked relatively untouched.

All of this gave Rick information about the enemy. Why would they bring them here to this supposedly uninhabited place in the middle of nowhere? He looked at the map Kruse had given him.

"Landing sites on the north side, near the northeast peninsula," he said.

"Are we sure we even want to go there?" Healy asked. "What if it's a trap?"

"Let's face it; it doesn't really matter either way. If it's a trap, then we're fucked. We're fucked for sure if we try and make a run for it. You think they don't have eyes on us?"

"True, I guess," Healy said. *Oh, I was so happy to be out of the service. No longer having to deal with being killed.*

"He said there'd be supplies and instructions waiting for us. And people. So, let's not get too excited if we see anyone there."

"You say that like there's nothing to be excited about already," Ranch said. Belville steered the boat to port, keeping a hundred feet from the rocks. For several hundred yards, the shore was nothing but rocks and low hanging trees. Landing a boat here would be impossible.

"You sure this is the way, Rick?" Shaw asked.

"Just a little further," Rick said.

"We sure they aren't just jerking us around?" Healy said.

"I'm sure they didn't go through all this effort just to have us circling the island nonstop," Rick said.

They went on for another hundred meters, watching the trees passing by. Some stood well over a hundred feet, containing bright green leaves of all shapes and sizes.

"There it is." Rick pointed at a small wooden dock located in a small cove on the right. The cove was void of any large rocks, and led to a small grey beach. A dozen feet inland was a twelve-foot raft, though nobody was in sight.

"I'd say it's a safe bet that the rest of our 'party' as Kruse calls it, came in on that," Belville said.

"Probably dropped off by that plane," Shaw added.

"Or maybe more mercenaries," Ranch speculated.

"Doubt it," Rick said.

"Just wishful thinking, I guess. I'm eager to shoot one of those pricks," Ranch muttered.

"Bel, take us to shore," Rick said. Belville slowed the boat, keeping an eye on the water to make sure there were no rocks, or any other surprises under the hull. So far, there was nothing other than his own reflection.

He lined the boat up with the wooden dock. Rick was the first one to step up. He noticed that the wood was new, the silver screwheads emitting the sun's rays. This dock was a few days old at most. The shore behind it was a few dozen feet of knee-high grass leading to a wall of trees. Birds hopped from branch-to-branch. Monkeys called to one another, while mosquitoes began buzzing out of the low canopy.

Belville and Healy secured the Zodiac to the dock, while Ranch and Shaw followed Rick to the shore. Other than the wildlife, there was no movement.

That worried Rick more than anything. He followed the tree line to the left then stopped. The men behind him saw his raised fist extend to an open hand, signaling for them to take cover.

Ranch groaned, instinctively reaching for a sidearm that wasn't there.

"See something, boss?" he asked.

"We're being watched," Rick calmly replied. He stepped forward, both hands in plain view. He watched a group of thick trees and bushes directly ahead of him. "I can hear you breathing in there!" he called. "We're unarmed. We're not a threat."

"Doesn't mean they aren't," Belville whispered.

"Either shoot me, or show yourself!" Rick said loudly. "DON'T make me fish you out!"

He heard the rustling of leaves and the barely audible crunching of footsteps. Finally, a figure, dressed in the same gear as themselves, emerged from the trees, pointing the muzzle of an M4 Carbine at Rick's face. Rick instantly recognized his crooked nose, angular jaw, and high cheekbones behind the iron sights.

"Atkins!" Rick said, making sure to be loud enough for the team to overhear.

"Rick Eilerman!" Atkins exclaimed, lowering the weapon. The two slapped hands.

"Holy shit," Ranch said. "They got you too."

Atkins tapped fists with the rest of his former team.

"Looks like you'll be sharing this shitty experience with me," he said. "I'm glad I held back. My first instinct was to blow away whoever was arriving on that Zodiac."

"I see you haven't changed a bit," Healy remarked. Atkins faked a grin at the half-joke. He turned back toward the woods and waved a hand.

"Ishmael! Zimmerman! Quit hiding in there. They're friendlies."

Two fellow mercenaries emerged from the jungle, one sporting an MP5, the other a Mossberg 500 pistol grip shotgun.

"Guys, this bastard here is my old squad leader, Rick Eilerman," Atkins introduced. The one with the submachine gun approached first.

"Pleasure, sir. Call me Ishmael," he said. He was a tall individual, almost as tall as Belville, though not as heavily built.

"Good pickup line," Rick replied, shaking his hand. The other one stepped forward. His eyes moved up and down, sizing Rick up. "I'm assuming you're Zimmerman?"

"You must be a fucking genius," Zimmerman replied. He spoke with a thick Cockney accent.

"SAS?" Rick said.

"For a time. I didn't see eye-to-eye with them. If it were up to me, that Zodiac would've been blown out of the water before it even got close."

Rick glanced over at Atkins, then back at Zimmerman.

"I can see why Atkins hired you."

"So, what's your story?" Ranch said. "Did they seek you guys out and ambush you?"

Atkins bit his lip and shrugged. "I hate to admit it, but we walked right into their hands. They used one of our normal contacts to get in touch with us. Same contact who'd arranged over two dozen jobs for us in the last year or so. These assholes who sent us here, they must've paid the prick off."

"Won't do him much good once we get ahold of him," Zimmerman added.

"Basically, we arrived in Seattle for a private meeting," Atkins continued. "Same place, same time as usual. Walk into the guy's garage, and before we're through the door, all three of us are hit with sedative darts. Barely caught a glimpse of the guys that did it. I hate to admit it, but of all of us, we were probably the easiest to catch."

"Woke up in a damn plane," Zimmerman said with a sneer. "With nothing. They took our weapons. Our gear. Made us dress in this cheap shit. The plane landed, and they pushed us out on that raft over there."

Healy glanced at the H&K and Mossberg.

"I see you have weapons now."

"There's a crate just beyond the bend back there," Atkins said, nudging his head over his left shoulder. "There's a few M4s, some MP5s, some grenades, Beretta nine-millimeters among other supplies."

"Well, don't mind me," Ranch said, brushing by the others as he made his way to the bend. The rest of the group followed, with Rick and Atkins walking beside each other.

"Did they say anything about us when they dropped you off?"

"They told us others would be coming, though they didn't state who or why," Atkins said. "There's an audio tape by the weapons, but we didn't get a chance to listen to it. We heard your boat, and we wanted to make sure we had the drop on you in case you were by chance a threat. You?"

"They just gave us this map of the island." Rick unfolded the satellite image and presented it.

"No markers other than here," Atkins said. "I suppose we'll find out more when we listen to that audiotape."

"You have any clue who these guys are? Or what they want?" Shaw asked.

Atkins shook his head. "No. Never met them. Didn't recognize any of the hired guns they were using."

"Seeing as that's your line of work, you ever hear of anyone in the business going by the name of Kruse?" Rick asked.

Atkins' head perked up. "Pasty-faced fella. About this high?" He raised his hand a couple of inches over Rick's brow.

"Yeah, that's him."

"He's former Army. 75th Battalion," Atkins said. "Thought to be dead back in '04. Went missing for a couple of years, or so we thought. Turns out the Army was burying a story. I guess he went rogue after his CO got a couple of his buddies killed. Put a round between the sorry bastard's eyes, then went all *Rambo* in a Taliban controlled village. Went in there for the terrorists, but also killed several locals in the process. Since then, he's been off the grid. You think he's the one behind this?"

"No," Rick said. "But he's working for whoever is."

"We'll pay him a special visit too, once we find a way out of here," Ishmael said. Rick resisted making any remarks. These mercenaries clearly had egos that could scale Mt. Everest. Such ego in a situation like this never produced good results.

"Whoever *is* behind this, they've got a beef with Fireteam Delta. It's no coincidence all of us were brought here together," Rick said.

"I wasn't part of your old unit. Nor was Ishmael," Zimmerman said.

"Did you go to the meeting with Atkins?" Rick asked, already impatient with Zimmerman's cockiness. The merc nodded. "It was him they were after. You guys just happened to be in the wrong place at the wrong time, and now you're stuck in this shitshow with us."

"Fair enough," Zimmerman said.

The group traveled along the grassy shoreline, then passed a grouping of boulders. Behind them was a small clearing where the supply crate was located. Weapon cases had been separated and opened, with several fully loaded magazines set nearby.

Ranch had already holstered a Beretta and was in the process of inspecting one of the Mossberg shotguns.

"Any of you mercenaries test these weapons out?"

Zimmerman glanced up at an albatross flying in from the ocean. He pointed his Mossberg and fired a shot. A red mist exploded from the bird, which spiraled down to the island.

"Satisfied?" he said.

"A simple 'Yes' would've sufficed," Ranch said. Zimmerman grinned then strutted past him. Ranch had half a mind to make a go at the prick, but he noticed the disapproving look from Rick. *Fine.*

Rick grabbed an M4 and slammed a magazine in place, then grabbed one of the H&Ks and slung it over his shoulder. After loading and holstering a sidearm, he picked up the other M4 and handed it to Shaw. Belville grabbed a Mossberg, while Healy grabbed one of the MP5s. There were sixteen grenades, which were divided equally between the eight men.

Belville found the recording device, which was propped up on a rock. The others gathered around it. Belville pressed the *play* button. For several seconds, they heard only white noise in the background.

"You are probably all curious why you are here."

"No shit," Ranch muttered, only to be shushed by Rick.

"I will get right to the point. You have been chosen to complete a task. By now, you have likely armed yourselves with the weapons provided. Your task is simple, but not easy. There is a fugitive here on this island with you. Hunt him down and kill him. Plain and simple. You're obviously questioning this objective right now, which is understandable."

The men exchanged glances with one another. Nobody recognized the voice. It was male, slightly husky, giving them the impression of someone in their forties. Whoever it was, it was well-spoken with no stutters.

"Your target has been a subject of genetic experimentation. To put it frank, he's been modified to have superior strength, superior intellect, stealth, stamina, and everything else that makes a perfect soldier. We want you to kill him. If you can. Failure to comply will result in the death of Ashley Rhee. Success will grant her freedom, and a sum of one million dollars paid to all survivors. Any attempt to leave this island will result in Mrs. Rhee's death, as well as your own. Take my word for it: your best hope of survival is to successfully complete this objective. You have the advantage in numbers and firepower."

Ranch looked over at Rick, whispering "The fuck?"

"Your target does not tire. Needs little rest. He is always planning for his next kill. And he is out there now, waiting for you. Complete your objective and bring the body back to this location, after which you will be returned Stateside with your payment. I would take this seriously if I

were you—your lives, and Mrs. Rhee's, depend on it. You have until nightfall. If the objective is not complete by sundown, consider this island your new permanent residence."

The recorder switched off. The group stood in stunned silence, absorbing what they had just heard.

Zimmerman broke the silence with a high-pitched laugh.

"Mates, I've seen some weird shit. That takes the cake!"

"Quit treating this like it's a joke," Rick said.

"You're going to believe shit about super-soldiers?"

"I know we're in over our heads—and that they didn't bring us here for no reason," Rick said.

"I doubt they utilized all these resources just so they could play a joke on us," Ranch added.

"I agree with you," Atkins said. "But something's not adding up. Why *us?* They cherry-picked us: Fireteam Delta, 3rd Battalion, 7th Marines. They picked US. Why?"

Rick took a breath. "I don't know. I didn't recognize that voice."

"Nor do I," Ranch said. "Nor do I believe this bullshit about a million bucks."

"All eight of us, against one guy?" Belville added. "He said he was a fugitive, but there was no elaboration on that. They could've hired *anyone* to take out a fugitive. And whoever this guy is, why is he out in the middle of nowhere?"

"You think there's an ulterior motive?" Ishmael asked.

"It's obvious," Belville replied.

"Genetic experiments; not hiring a full mercenary team or active duty strike force—I don't think they're looking to outright kill this fella," Rick said.

"What do you think it is?" Healy said.

"I think this is a test," Rick replied. "A live-fire exercise. Whoever's out there, assuming it's one person, he's as aware of us as we are of him. For all we know, he's just beyond those trees watching us right now."

Atkins shook his head. "That still doesn't explain why they chose *us*."

"No, it doesn't," Rick admitted.

Several more moments of silence passed. Zimmerman looked at the former marines, then shook his head.

"Fuck this. I say we just take a boat and get out of here."

Rick spun to face him, having already had his fill of the merc's attitude.

"Where you going to go? You don't even know where you are."

"Fuck it. I'll just head east. Bound to hit land at some point."

"Unless you run out of fuel first," Ranch said. "I thought you SAS guys were smart."

"Probably why he got kicked out," Belville said. Zimmerman turned left, his eyes burning into the large marine. Belville saw the aggressive stance and swiftly stepped up to him. He stood five inches over the merc, ready to grab him by the throat and toss him into the ocean. Belville had to give the prick a little credit; most people usually backed down in these moments.

"Settle down," Rick ordered. "Listen. I agree, something about this doesn't add up. I can't even say that they'll let us out of this alive even if we do kill this fugitive. But I do know that they have Ashley Rhee, and I'm not going to risk her life by letting anyone attempt to flee the island."

"So…what?" Zimmerman replied. "You gonna go on a mighty man-hunt? Kill the *perfect soldier*?"

"Zimmerman, shut the fuck up," Atkins said. Zimmerman brushed a hand over his four-day beard then stepped away, muttering a few curse words. Atkins shook his head disapprovingly, then looked at his former Sergeant. "He's a good soldier. Really good at hacking databases and bypassing security systems. It's just…the life's just got to him."

"Oh, really? I couldn't tell," Ranch said.

"Listen, Atkins," Rick said. "I suggest we all work together. It's our best chance to survive. If we leave, we're dead."

"You think they're watching?" Ishmael asked. Rick pointed his thumb forty-five degrees over his shoulder. All eyes went to the large tree behind him, and saw the black camera mounted beneath one of the high branches.

Ranch immediately held his middle finger at it.

"Well, shit," Zimmerman muttered.

"What do you suggest?" Ishmael asked. Rick turned to the right and began walking for the northeast peninsula.

"We start by searching the coastlines," he said.

"The coastlines?!" Ishmael exclaimed. "Aren't we on a time-limit? If we don't put this fella down by dark, we're never getting out of here. I say we plow right into the island and seek this bastard out. He won't be hiding around on the coastlines, I'll tell you that."

"I wanna know more about where we're at," Rick replied. "Let's check the peninsula, then work our way around to the cliffs on the southwest." He walked a few steps, then glanced back at the men. "You coming?"

Atkins watched his former teammates hustle to follow him. The two subordinates looked at him with questioning eyes.

"It's up to you, sir," Ishmael said. Zimmerman said nothing, though a condescending scoff could be heard from the back of his throat.

"Come on. Let's go," Atkins said.

CHAPTER 10

The journey to the northeast peninsula took the group over jagged ground composed of rocks, plants, and disgusting insect nests. Tall grass swatted against the men's thighs, while bugs rained down from above like attack helicopters. The group stayed along the perimeter, keeping away from the thick of the jungle, while cautiously keeping an eye on it.

The peninsula was an enormous hill overlooking the ocean. The final hundred feet was a steep slope that led down to a rocky shore.

Rick watched the waves crash against the rocks. There was nothing there but grass and a few scattered trees. The group waited for their next instruction, many of them looking longingly out into the ocean.

"Is this the Atlantic or Pacific?" Zimmerman asked. To Rick's surprise, and pleasure, the hothead seemed to have cooled down a bit.

"Definitely the Pacific," Rick said. He pointed at a plant behind Zimmerman. "See those shrubs. That's a Fijian Fire Plant. Doesn't grow on any Atlantic Ocean islands. Judging by some of the animal life around here, we're definitely somewhere off the coast of South America."

"Be nice if we could see it," Healy said. He gazed far out into the ocean. There wasn't a patch of land anywhere in sight. As far as they were concerned, this tiny little island was their world.

Atkins' gaze pierced the jungle. Every branch, every bush seemed to have a life of its own. Every movement caught his eye. Monkeys passed along the branches overhead, curiously watching the men in black. The jungle was thick, but passable. Still, his line of sight ended at a little over a hundred feet. The animal calls were a constant assault on the ears. It was peaceful and relaxing, while simultaneously foreboding. The worst part was that it concealed any movement caused by anyone lurking out there.

Already, the waiting and anticipation was getting to him.

"Let's keep going," Rick said. "We'll head south from here and work our way along the shore to the cliffs."

"I think that's a waste of time," Atkins said. Rick closed his eyes, taking a moment to bury his frustration.

"This is our safest bet," Rick said.

"Nothing about this is *safe*," Atkins said. "Ishmael was right. If we're supposed to be hunting somebody, we won't find him out along the island perimeter. He'll be in there somewhere. I say we push into the jungle and search for clues. We've all had tracking experience. Belville is REALLY good at it, from what I remember. Right Bel?"

Belville didn't take the bait, though he wasn't fully against the thought either.

"I agree with the Sarge. We don't know who we're up against," he replied. Atkins could tell he wasn't fully convinced in that statement. The scientist's remark about being done by nightfall was textbook manipulation—because it worked, regardless of whether or not it was true. Was anyone here ready to risk that? Atkins wasn't, nor were his two mercenaries, and he suspected most of the team, despite their loyalty to Rick, were keen on the possibility of remaining here permanently.

"We keep moving along the perimeter," Rick said. "We'll get a better scope of the layout that way."

"We have a map," Ishmael said. He spoke neutrally with no combativeness, not intending to stir discourse.

"You trust anything those guys gave us?" Ranch replied.

"The weapons seem to work," Zimmerman said.

"True. But we still don't know who we're up against. And if he knows we're here, he's got the advantage."

"Eight against one? I say we have the advantage," Shaw said.

Rick could feel his blood pressure rising. Shaw was a good marine, but he did have a hankering for rushing headfirst into a conflict. There were many missions where Rick had to reaffirm that his strategy had a cut and clear purpose, which led him to sometimes explain things in laymen terms.

"He's probably been here for years, as far as we know. He knows every crook, every tree, every ravine. He knows where to ambush us," Rick said. "We also don't know what weapons he has, if any."

"Another reason why I don't want to be in the open," Atkins said. Rick reminded himself that he was not talking with a subordinate, but a gun-for-hire leading his own men. Atkins was not going to unquestionably follow Rick's instructions. And by the looks of it, his two mercenaries were going to back him up. Rick had to be diplomatic, rather than bullheaded. The last thing he needed was hot tensions within the group.

"We need to be on our guard, you're right. But we need a better understanding of this place before we do anything. We have plenty of cover out here. There's enough trees and boulders to take refuge behind, should the need arise. It's not like we've landed in a drop-zone evaluated by Central Intelligence, with a marked target with a known number of security forces and weaponry. We're in the middle of nowhere. We're *lost*. I suggest we keep going around the island."

"We're gonna have to go in there at some point," Atkins said.

"We will when we're better prepared," Rick said. "If we go in there now, we're as good as dead." He shouldered his M4 and started walking south. Atkins reluctantly followed, only to be stopped by Healy and Ranch.

"You know he's right," Ranch said. "If you go rushing in there, you could get yourself and the rest of us killed."

"Oh really?" Atkins said. "I see you're conveniently forgetting what happened in Haraz…and what happened to Danny Rhee."

"Oh, Jesus, Angelo. You're seriously not gonna hang that over his head," Ranch said.

"Believe what you want. He made the plan, and *I* warned him against it. In front of everyone. Still, he went in there, and Danny died as a result."

Ranch shook his head, then turned away, frustrated. Healy glanced back at the former Sergeant, who marched a couple of hundred feet along the edge of the hill. He leaned in toward Atkins.

"I think Rick's right."

"You think that, but you also have doubts," Atkins said. Healy offered no argument. The medic was split down the middle. He trusted Rick's judgement, but also felt like they needed to engage the threat directly. One thing was for certain; he no longer had the physical or mental endurance for these kinds of situations. Like many of the others, he had settled into civilian life with no intention of looking back. Atkins could see it in his eyes, and also in the way he stood. Healy had mentioned onset of arthritis in their last few months together. He could tell by his body language when not walking that his joints were pestering him. Healy always seemed to be on the lookout for something to lean or sit on. And this was only the beginning.

The mercenary watched the jungle, combing every twisted shape with his eyes. His gaze returned to the medic.

"While I don't agree with Rick, I am against splitting up," he said. "We'll keep going. But sooner or later, we'll have to press inward. And that might be sooner than what Rick's willing to do."

Ishmael stepped alongside him.

"You really think there's just one guy we're hunting?"

"Can't really tell by just studying the perimeter," Atkins said. "Though, I'll admit that it's strange we haven't found a sizable dock for personnel to arrive. And there were no other boats back where we all arrived. To know for sure, we'll need to go toward the center of the island."

"Not like we've never been in a jungle before," Ishmael said.

"No, it's not," Atkins said. "Still, I'd like to get Belville on our side. He's an excellent tracker—one of the best I've seen."

A sharp whistle from Rick caught their attention. All three men recognized the stare, and the message that came with it. *You coming?*

"Let's go," Atkins said softly. Healy and Ishmael hurried along, joining the others behind Rick. The group kept a few yards apart, each man keeping a watchful eye on their counterpart, while also watching the jungle.

Atkins gave one last look to the north before hustling to catch up.

A rustling of leaves startled him into a half-firing stance. Something had moved between the bushes, and it was no breeze. Atkins poised, slipping his finger into the trigger guard. He gave a quick glance to the others, who were now a couple of hundred feet to his left.

If this was the target, it was seeking him out directly.

Good, come and get me you little fucker. He proceeded to study the situation as though the target's presence was confirmed. If there was someone watching from behind that wall of jungle dead ahead, then he was likely aware that Atkins was watching.

Atkins was no stranger to using himself as bait. If the target was armed, then he would've already picked him off by now. There was no other movement yet, meaning he hadn't retreated back into the jungle.

He inched his way into the trees. A horrid stench assaulted his nostrils. Atkins wasn't sure what it was. Hell, it was the jungle, it could be anything—even a diversion.

He didn't want to give the enemy a moment to plan. Atkins rushed toward the bushes, trigger half-pressed. He sprinted the twenty-foot distance, then saw the monkey bursting out of the bushes. It scurried up a tree, with a long green lizard tail dangling from its mouth. It looked back at Atkins with large, buggy eyes, then proceeded into the canopy.

The mercenary caught his breath.

"Fucking monkey," he said. He glanced into the jungle. *At least I know it wasn't the so-called fugitive.*

Atkins hurried back toward the perimeter and followed the rest of the group. Together, they proceeded down the east side of the hill, which led to a rocky shoreline. From there, they continued south.

The foolish human was so close. Another few steps, and it would've been within its grasp. Its jaws mashed the lower half of the iguana it had killed moments prior, whose tail was picked off by the furry scavenger.

The creature stood up on its hind legs, savoring the blood of its victim. Each mashing motion of its jaw furthered its desire to kill. It stayed close to the trees, watching the group through the gaps between them. There were eight, each armed with deadly firearms. Memories flashed in its mind. It remembered the loud cracks, the recoil from discharge, the look on someone's face when shooting.

It knew it couldn't engage with these humans out in the open. It would get two, maybe three before being overwhelmed by the firepower. It would have to bide its time. It was only a matter of time before one strayed from the group.

Its claws curled at the thought of ripping limbs from body and flesh from bone. Its thin white lips peeled back, revealing a toothy smile, dripping with lizard blood.

To its left, the monkey came scurrying down the tree, not thinking anything of the humanoid creature. It still carried the stolen lizard tail from its mouth. In a blur of motion, the creature's curved claw found its neck. The tail went twirling far out into the jungle, still clenched in the monkey's jaws. Its body, however, fell at the creature's feet, spurting blood between the shoulders.

CHAPTER 11

The eastern shore was nothing but an endless line of razor-sharp rocks. Stretching the two-mile length from the tip of the peninsula to the southeast coast, these jagged formations looked like the teeth of an enormous beast that was ready to rise up from the Pacific and swallow the island whole.

The jungle was denser along the shoreline, forcing the team to weave between groupings of trees and thick bushes as they went along. As the jungle thickened, they tightened their group formation, making sure that nobody got separated from the group.

Every step was taken with caution. With the grass being so long, it was easy for someone to conceal a tripwire along their path. Flies buzzed around their heads, aggravating the already stressed group. A soft breeze passed from the south, carrying with it a hot stench.

Rick knew something was off about this area. The flies, the smell— he was reminded of the mass graves he and his team discovered in Samaria. He saw the sentiment in the facial expressions of his team members, including Atkins.

Not a single word was spoken as they continued on for another few hundred yards. Finally, they came to a stretch of shoreline void of trees. However, the rocks had almost doubled in number. Large black masses were embedded in the sand like Normandy obstacles. Rick led the group around these huge rocks.

As they went, the stench increased, as did the number of bugs. Also, there were many birds flying low, just a couple of hundred feet ahead. Something was attracting the wildlife here.

Using hand signals, Rick ordered the team to branch out and for those in the rear to provide cover fire for a possible encounter. Atkins and his mercenaries spread three meters apart and took one-knee firing positions, with the leader cautiously watching the forest.

Rick continued forward, with the rest of the team following closely behind. They stepped around a large, hook-shaped rock, then gazed at the stretch of beach behind it. Frightened seagulls took to the air like one gigantic white cloud, leaving a large brown mass laying beneath them. At first glance, it looked like another large boulder. It was certainly almost as big.

Then they noticed the large head and well-developed mane, and the thick globs of blood soaking the sand around it.

Rick lowered his rifle muzzle.

"A South American sea lion," he said. They approached the dead thing. It was fully grown, weighing over four-hundred pounds. Its head was facing the group, mouth partially agape. The rest of the group followed him as he approached.

It was when they gathered around the carcass that they noticed that its throat was slashed. Worse, its entire underside had been torn completely open. There was almost no skin or muscle tissue from the breast to the pelvic area. Everything inside had been mashed, as though placed in a giant blender. Shreds of tissue had spilled into the sand, intestines trailing behind it with the tide.

Stranger yet was the sight of four other dead sea lions scattered across the beach. Three of them were females, thrice the size of their male counterparts.

"The fuck happened here?" Ranch said. They gathered around the large male with the split-open underside. Healy took a look, then winced.

"I don't suppose there are tigers in the Pacific..." Shaw said.

"Even a tiger would have a rough time taking down one of these bad boys," Healy said. "Something got ahold of this guy and tore him up."

"Don't males battle for dominance?" Zimmerman asked.

"To my knowledge, they don't tear each other up like this," Rick said.

"This is weirder than that," Healy added. "Look at the insides! They're all messed up. Like something went in with a buzz-saw and ripped it to shreds. The stomach, lungs, they're all torn out."

"Maybe a shark got it," Shaw suggested.

"That'd be one hell of a big shark," Healy said. "Contrary to the movies, even a great white would have a hard time going after a fella this big."

"And it doesn't explain the throat wounds," Rick added. He knelt down and pointed at the sea lion's neck. There were three slash marks, several inches deep, running parallel across. "Whatever did this, it knew how to make a killing blow. Though, most animals that know to go for the throat usually bite, not slash."

"And what about these?" Ishmael said. He walked along the beach, looking at the dead females. One had her head completely ripped off and tossed to the side. It rolled with the tide, several feet from its body. Loose red flesh dangled in thick flaps where their throats used to be. Similar slash marks riddled their bodies. Their eyes had been gouged out, leaving two red holes leading deep into their skulls.

The second male was even larger than the first. Its left shoulder was nothing but red blubber with no skin to cover it. Judging by the number of slash marks, and the mounds of sand all around it, this male put up the biggest fight against whatever invaded their beach.

Rick grimaced at the huge wound on the back of the male's head. A whole section of its skull had been broken away, exposing the pinkish brain matter inside. The wound was the size of a football, with coarse edges that gave it the appearance of a bite mark. Its flippers had been slashed to ribbons, as had its legs and belly.

"That's no bullet wound," he said. "There has to be some kind of animal on this island."

"What kind of animal would slaughter prey like this but not eat it?" Belville asked.

"I don't know. I'm no zoologist," Rick said. "But whatever did this, did it up close and personal. You can see the signs of a struggle."

"Yeah, and it didn't happen very long ago," Belville added. "The tide would've smoothened the sand after a day." He knelt down to inspect the ground. The group backed up to let him search for clues.

"You think it's even possible to find anything?" Zimmerman asked.

"That guy would find fly shit in pepper," Rick answered. It didn't take long for Belville to find something.

"Here!" he said. The group carefully approached and gazed at the section of sand the tracker had isolated. The shape was vague, partially washed away by the tide. Belville unsheathed his knife and carefully traced the shape to make it more visible for the others.

"A footprint?" Atkins said.

"Looks human," Ranch said.

"Don't know any humans with only four toes…which also look like eagle talons," Zimmerman said.

"Bel, you can track, but I'm not sure you can draw," Shaw said.

"I'm telling you, that's the shape," Belville said. He stepped away, combing the shore for more prints. "How 'bout this one?"

The second print was a larger indent, maintaining much of its original shape. Like the other, it had the basic shape of a human foot, but with abnormalities that gave it the appearance of something reptilian or birdlike. Even the heel appeared pointed, as though a fifth toe protruded out from it like the spur from the back of a boot.

"Anybody here an expert on animal life?" Ishmael said.

"I never heard of anything that made prints like that," Zimmerman said.

"Some Asian birds can be pretty large," Shaw pointed out.

"That's not a bird print," Zimmerman said.

"It's definitely not human," Healy said. As they stared at the print, Healy's eyes traced the sand behind it and spotted another one. "Whatever caused it, it came in from the jungle. Probably ambushed these poor things."

"Maybe a species of primate?" Ishmael said.

"Unlikely," Atkins replied. "Besides, no primate can inflict those types of wounds on those sea lions. Whatever slashed their throats were edged weapons."

A long silence came over the group. All they had were more questions and no answers.

"This has something to do with that recorder," Ranch said.

"You're buying that shit about genetic experimentation?" Zimmerman said. A sardonic smile began taking form over his face.

"I'm not sure," Ranch said. "It's the only thing that points to some sort of answer."

"I'm still not falling for it," Zimmerman said. He cocked his head to the side to into the jungle. "What's your tracker doing over there?"

Rick turned to look. Belville had moved a couple of hundred feet into the forest and was kneeling at a grassy area, examining the ground. The rest of the group quickly caught up with him.

"Bel, don't go wandering off," Rick said, in a stern voice. Belville didn't respond. His hands had peeled away many layers of grass, exposing the thick soil underneath. "You find something?"

"Take a look for yourself," Belville said. He ripped away some of the grass to make for a clearer view. There were faint signs of tread marks embedded in the ground. They were barely visible. Even at a close viewing, had Belville not pointed them out, they'd be nearly impossible to see.

Atkins stood beside Rick as he knelt to inspect the track marks.

"Told you we'd find clues," Rick said.

"Bulldozer? Backhoe? What did it? And when? Those tracks could be a year old for all we know," Atkins replied.

"It was definitely a heavy construction vehicle, or something of equal size," Belville said. He pointed into the forest. "See those trees?

See the discoloration in the bark? I think they were chipped by a bulldozer blade, or something similar. Whatever the case, something big was driven through this jungle, then left to sit here long enough to make a lasting imprint in the soil.

Could've been lifted out by helicopter once the job was complete."

"Right, and it tells us nothing," Atkins said.

"It tells us somebody was building something," Rick said.

"Whatever they were doing, they did it a while ago," Belville said. "First of all, these tread marks are barely visible. Two; you can see that the trees have long since healed. Also, if you look at the shrubs, you can tell they're much smaller than all the others. Because they've been crushed and regrown."

Several group members nodded.

"So, they've built something," Zimmerman said. "What exactly? A private home? A casino?"

"They certainly weren't building a dock or harbor," Ranch said.

"No. Whatever it was, it was built inland," Rick said. "And judging by the placement, and thickness of this jungle, they wanted to keep it obscured from plain view."

A thought struck Atkins' mind. He pointed a finger to Rick's vest pocket.

"That map of yours is a satellite image, right? Pull it out. Maybe we'll see something. If there's any facility, of any size, we'd be able to spot a gap in the canopy. We can pinpoint the location."

Rick grabbed the map and unfolded it. He and Atkins looked over the image, while the others kept watch. They scoured every square inch of the satellite photo. Nothing.

"Son of a bitch," Atkins muttered. "I was sure we had a clue."

"Probably an old photo," Shaw said.

"No, I don't think so," Rick said. "You can see the dock on the north side. If we can see that, then we'd definitely see a facility."

Atkins shouldered his rifle. "I say we follow the markings and see what we find."

"I'm not sure if that's a good idea," Rick said.

"This was your idea. *You* specifically stated you wanted to find clues," Atkins said.

Belville stepped forward. "Sarge, if you want, I can easily follow the trail. I don't think they meant for us to find this. This might work to our advantage. But it's up to you."

Rick considered it for a moment. He stared into the jungle, then looked back to the shoreline. Something about going into the jungle didn't feel right, especially after seeing those dead sea lions. His gaze returned to the thick wilderness. There was the odd, creeping feeling as though he was being watched. However, Atkins was right; they did find some kind of evidence that might lead to something.

"Alight. Everyone, pay attention. We'll investigate. Let's keep this simple. Keep a tight formation and everyone pay attention to your surroundings. Watch your footing, and be careful. This jungle, and every moving thing in it, will fuck with your eyes. I have a feeling whatever we're hunting is counting on that."

"You think it's a *what*, not a *who*?" Atkins said.

"I don't know what I think," Rick said.

The team separated into two four-man wedge formations, with Belville taking the lead of the front group. Any trace of tread marks became nearly invisible after three hundred feet. The jungle thickened, each waving branch drawing the attention of the fire teams.

Belville focused on the plant life conditions. He saw broken branches and crushed shrubs, now turned white from decomposition. The vehicle had passed through here at some point.

They kept going, stopping once every minute to observe their surroundings, particularly the wildlife. Any distress in the bird population could indicate a hostile presence.

The landscape was like a tidal wave of endless peaks. No two steps were even with one another. Not only did the group members have to watch for potential traps, but now they had to contend with the natural hazards of the island itself. Additionally, he worried about species of poisonous insects or spiders that could be lurking in the canopy, or even poisonous plants.

An ear-piercing screech caused each of them to drop to firing positions. Gun barrels swept the forest, ready to unleash hell's fury on anything that dared to emerge behind that blockade of trees.

They heard another screech, this time from above. The swinging of branches caught the group's attention, and they saw two monkeys wrestling with each other over a piece of fruit.

"Jesus," Rick said under his breath, simultaneously relieved and frustrated.

The group continued forward.

"This way," Belville said, pointing his shotgun barrel ten degrees to the right. The path took them over a trail of crushed shrubs and bushes, which then led to a cleared-out section of forest. Trees had been cut into sections and left to rot, providing thirty feet of clear open space. In the center of it all was a steel container, roughly ten feet long, five feet wide.

"The hell is that?" Ranch said.

"They cleared out a space just for this?" Atkins said. "A tiny metal box. Looks like a tiny shipping container."

"More like an elevator unit," Rick said. He carefully approached it. The front of the box had a mechanical door that was left wide open. There were no buttons inside or out. "Whatever this thing is, it was opened remotely."

"Yeah? I don't see any receiver," Atkins said.

"Unless this thing has a wired connection," Rick said.

"Wired to what? There's nothing here," Ishmael said. "Hell, this thing could be a hundred years old for all we know."

"It could be just a coincidence, Sarge," Shaw said.

"You think THAT is a coincidence?" Rick pointed to a tree. The group looked and spotted the camera he was looking at. "Or this?!" He yanked the door open wider, providing a clear view of the interior. Numerous abrasions lined the walls, mostly in streaks of three. Immediately, their minds flashed to the dead sea lions.

"I don't think this is a man we're hunting," Rick said.

"You think they've engineered an animal?" Zimmerman said. There was still a touch of doubt in his voice, though not to the same extent as before.

"A highly intelligent and VIOLENT animal," Rick emphasized. "One that is not afraid to attack something larger than itself...like those sea lions. I think this thing, whatever it is, is being tested. And *we're* the lab rats. It's obvious they WANT us to try and kill it—that's why they armed us."

"Then where is it?" Shaw said. "All I've seen are birds and monkeys."

"And dead sea lions," Zimmerman added.

"If it only kills in close quarters, then we have a great advantage," Atkins said, keeping his voice low enough not to be heard by anyone outside the group. "Assuming it's an *it* and not a *who*. I say we continue into the jungle and hunt it down."

Rick shook his head.

"That's suicide."

"Not if I'm right," Atkins said. "If we're dealing with an unarmed person...or animal, whatever you want to believe it is, we have a superior advantage. Belville can find clues, which'll allow us to track it down, corner it, then blow it away."

"I think that's what it wants us to do," Rick said. "I think we're falling into a trap. We need to head back to the beach, where we have a decent line of sight. We can develop a game plan, but we need more information."

"Oh, right," Atkins scoffed. "You'd rather have us patrol the island perimeter."

"For now, yes," Rick replied.

"Right. Let's waste more time," Atkins said.

"This wasn't a waste of time," Ranch snarled. "We've found clues to whatever it is we're dealing with."

"Yeah. We found a cage and some dead seals. With a bulldozer trail that looks to be a few years old."

"It's connected to whatever's going on," Rick said. "Look here. There's a metal platform under the box." He scraped away some of the dirt with his knife, revealing that the structure went further into the ground.

"So, now you're saying it's an underground elevator?" Atkins said.

"Possibly," Rick said.

"On a deserted island, with no evidence of heavy construction," Atkins said. "Rick, I don't have a grudge against you. I really don't. But I think your judgement has waned since…" He stopped, shook his head, deciding not to finish that sentence.

"Since…what? Go ahead. Say it."

Atkins stared off into the jungle. He didn't agree with Rick, but arguing over past events wasn't going to help the situation any.

"Never mind," he said. He turned to face his former Sergeant. "Okay, Eilerman, we'll do it your way. We'll circle the perimeter, look for whatever clues you want. But I'm telling you, man, you're wrong. I assure you, you are very wrong."

The two men glared into each other's eyes, until Rick stepped away.

"Back to the beach. Bel, lead the way," he said.

"Yes, sir." Belville spoke softly, failing to hide the sense of doubt in his voice. He agreed with Rick on most things, but on this one, he was starting to view things Atkins' way. He knew he could find clues to the whereabouts of the 'resident'. Plus, they had only a handful of hours before dark. It was early afternoon now and they had maybe seven hours to search. It was a small island, but combing a thick jungle like this for a single target, with only eight men, could take days.

He forced the thoughts aside and took first point.

CHAPTER 12

Flesh colored fluid dribbled on the woolly monkey's brown fur coat as it clung to the branch with its legs and prehensile tail. Clinging to the side of its branch, the fifteen-pound primate split the papaya open, revealing the orange fruit inside. It wasted no time gorging on the black seeds inside, before moving on to the orange fruit itself. It could hear the rest of its group nearby, scouring the other trees for fruit and the ground for invertebrates.

It ate the fruit and the skin, discarding a few unwanted bits before moving on to the next one. It jerked its head over its left shoulder at the sound of crackling branches. One of the other monkeys climbed up to join it. It snatched one of the papayas and split it open, while the first deliberately dropped one down for the others to find.

The fruit hit the ground and rolled like a soccer ball. Like a raging river, the monkeys converged on it. The largest pushed his way to the front and snatched the papaya from the hands of one of its smaller counterparts. The younger monkey stepped back, not daring to provoke the wrath of the dominant member of its group. But all was not lost. More papayas dropped down. The monkeys split them apart into slices, passing them among their members. Like a big family, they ate together, littering the forest floor with bits of skin.

One of them popped its head up to the sound of movement. It stood on its hind legs and scanned the surroundings with its eyes. Something was approaching. Others heard it too. It was a faint noise that could easily be missed, like a jaguar ducking under bushes to sneak up on its prey.

All at once, the monkeys ascended into the trees. In just a few moments, not one remained on the ground.

From high above, they watched the forest floor. They caught glimpses of its cement-colored hide as it passed behind a series of bushes. It stopped, then peeked around a curtain of low-hanging branches. Black eyes peered up at the group. The monkeys poised, ready to retreat deep into the jungle. The thing stood upright. Razor teeth lined its clenched jaws; definitely a predator.

After staring for a few moments, the thing continued on toward the southwest shoreline. They heard other animals scatter as it disappeared from view. The fact that it was out of sight gave the woolly monkeys little comfort. The leader was the first to move, taking a branch from the adjacent tree and moving on over to it.

The rest of the pack followed. There was always an opportunity to find other food. Right now, all that mattered was that they put distance between them and the horrid predator that lurked in the shadows.

CHAPTER 13

The journey around the back of the island was a literal uphill one. All the way from the southeast corner, the landscape elevated into a long cliff shelf that looked out into the Pacific. The one good thing the group had going for them was the fact that this edge of the island had few trees, allowing for clear line of sight. There were plenty of bushes with leaves as long as a human, and the grass stood up to their knees, but overall, the vegetation was sparse enough to prevent any ambush attacks. Still, the team was wary of any surprises the island might have, so they made sure to check every bush for anything possibly waiting inside.

They walked a mile and a half before reaching the southwest corner of the island. Rick absorbed the ocean breeze as he stood on the edge of the cliff. He was over two-hundred feet above the water. Looking straight down, he saw nothing but ocean. The cliff edge extended over the water like a shelf, obscuring the underside from any view up top.

They seized the opportunity to take a break. Ranch, Belville, and Shaw walked a few meters down, then took turns urinating while the others kept watch. Healy searched for a place to sit. His knees were aching. A year after getting out of the service, he first discovered he was developing some arthritis. In a few more years, he'd be looking at some knee replacements. He found a rock to sit on, but its rounded shape was hell on his aching back. Mentally, he recited the motto *'Once a marine, always a marine. There is no such thing as an ex-marine'*. The truth, however, was that he was not the young bull-headed fighter he used to be. Just the patrolling alone was killing him, and they hadn't even found the target yet.

The three mercenaries remained grouped together. Zimmerman was the most visibly frustrated of the bunch. Like Atkins, he believed the best course of action was to head straight into the jungle and complete the objective.

Rick could sense the rising tension in the group. There was a mounting feeling of anticipation. They had seen nothing up until now aside from the dead seals and the strange crate.

"Enjoying the view?" Zimmerman asked Rick.

"I'm thinking," he replied.

"Let me guess: the next course of action is to search the west shoreline."

"I'm considering it," Rick replied.

"Great," Healy muttered from the rock. He swallowed, not intending for his thought to actually be verbalized. With his posture on the rock wreaking havoc on his body, he stood up and walked north along the tall grass.

"You alright there, Corpsman?" Ranch said to him.

"Yeah, I'm fine," Healy said. Belville and Shaw completed their leaks, then positioned their weapons. Healy's physical ailments were no secret to the group. He barely got through his final year in the service. All the physical conditioning, endless missions, and stress was finally taking their toll on his body. He had complained of his aches during past gatherings at Ashley's place.

Belville turned to look at Shaw and Ranch.

"You guys know I trust the Sarge, but we can't keep circling the island like this," he said.

"You think we should follow Atkins?" Ranch said.

"I'm not saying he should lead the group. I'm just saying he might be right in this case. If there's someone here looking to kill us, he'll be waiting for us in there. He won't engage us out in the open like this."

"The Sarge is playing it safe right now," Ranch replied.

"Playing it safe is what's breaking us down," Healy chimed in. "This isn't a stroll through the park. This is an island filled with rolling hills, trees, rocks, no decent place to rest up. Look, one foot's higher than the other. Every step falls on uneven ground."

"You think it'll be any better in *there*?" Ranch pointed into the jungle.

"No," Healy said. "I just want to complete this task and get the hell off this island."

"I'm worried about Ashley," Shaw said. "You think those guys are serious about terminating her if we don't have this done by nightfall?"

"I don't see any reason not to believe them," Ranch admitted.

"Then we need to hurry up. By the looks of it, we've got maybe six hours to go. Why is the Sarge delaying?"

"He's keeping a clear head. Believe me, he wants to save her just as bad as the rest of us. But he's also keen on keeping us alive as well. It's a tough choice, but he's very good at making the right calls," Ranch said. "You know him. He's saved our asses a hundred times."

"Yeah, but those were all deployments with proper intel," Shaw said. "Ranch, I love the Sarge like a brother. Just like all of you. But this is different. I think he's afraid to push into the jungle."

"Of course, he is. Because he's SMART," Ranch said. "And what you just said about having intel; that's what he's doing—gathering whatever intel he can find before making a move. This isn't an infiltration on an enemy location in which they're not aware of our presence. I guarantee you, whoever we're hunting, knows we're here. And probably knows more about us than we do about him. If it's a *him*."

"Yeah, and that intel says that we're not going to find him hiding on the shore," Healy said.

Several yards back, the three mercenaries huddled together for a similar conversation.

"We're wasting time," Zimmerman said to his boss. "Perhaps we should just infiltrate the jungle and get this job done ourselves."

"No," Atkins said. "You're right about going in there, but separating isn't the way to do it. We have no radios; no means of communication."

"This guy's gonna get us killed," Ishmael said, pointing his thumb back at Rick. "From how it looks, we're gonna be circling this island all day."

"I think he's lost his edge since leaving the service. Got a little too cozy in civilian life," Zimmerman said. "He's afraid to go into that jungle."

"I don't care if we're hunting one guy, or twenty," Ishmael said. "We've faced worse odds in Bosnia, in worse conditions."

Atkins nodded. He saw Rick turn around. His former Sergeant gave him a menacing look, then proceeded to join up with the others. Atkins shook his head slightly condescendingly. He remembered Rick's keen sense of hearing. Good, let him listen—let him hear how everyone thought he was making the wrong call.

"Let's keep going," Rick said.

"For how long, sir?" Shaw asked.

"That tall peak a half-mile up, I wanna check it out." He pointed to a high elevation northward. It extended out over the ocean like a small peninsula.

"What's so special about it?" Atkins asked.

"It's not on the map," Rick said. The rest of the group gathered by him.

"What's going on, boss?" Ranch asked.

"This image has been tampered with," Rick said. He held the map out to show the group. "That peak over there. It's not on this image."

"That doesn't make sense. You're saying they gave us a map of the wrong island?" Ishmael said.

"The map is of this island," Rick said. "But they've tampered with the image. Look, you can see the peninsula is still there. There's the rocks on the east shoreline. The cliffs. The docks. But they've left *that* out."

"Rick, I think you're making a mountain out of a molehill. It's just part of the cliffs," Atkins said.

"No," Rick said. "That section is completely disconnected from the cliffs we're standing on now."

"Christ, Eilerman! We're supposed to be out hunting somebody, while you're standing there fiddling with a piece of paper," Atkins said.

"You can see the elevation with your own eyes," Rick said. "This ought to stand out on the map, but it doesn't. There's something there they didn't want us to find."

Zimmerman chuckled. "Like another crate?"

Healy sighed, then stepped forward. "Sir, with all due respect, but we've already got a shitload of unanswered questions. Who are these guys who brought us here? Who do they want us to kill? What the hell was in that crate?"

"Not only that, but we're on a time limit," Shaw added.

"Guys, knock it off," Ranch said. "The Sarge is on to something."

"Damn right I am," Rick said. "Let's go check it out. I want to know what's special about this place."

"It's not special. The clues that matter are in *there*," Atkins said, pointing at the jungle. Rick got in his face, so close that each man could count the blood vessels in each other's eyes.

"We don't know what we're up against. You lead us into that jungle, we're as good as dead."

"If we don't kill this guy by nightfall, we're stuck here," Atkins said. "You're taking a relatively easy task and making it difficult. Seems to be a habit with you. Remember Haraz? You wanted to clear the building exterior of hostiles before taking Danny down to the basement to complete the objective. I suggested you go right for it and allow the rest of us to provide cover. But no. You thought you were playing it safe. And look what happened."

Hot air blasted from Rick's nostrils. He let his rifle hang from its sling, while his hands balled up into fists. Collecting his emotions, he backed off.

"It was never going to be easy," he said. He turned and started walking toward the peak. Ranch was the first to follow. Belville and Shaw looked at each other, then at Healy. The medic pushed himself off the rock he was leaning on and marched up the hill, glancing back and forth between the ocean and jungle.

Atkins' fellow mercenaries watched Rick walk off, then turned their eyes toward their boss, waiting to see what he would do. They were loyal to him like bloodhounds, not willing to follow another leader unless Atkins himself did so. His patience with Rick was paper-thin at this point, and it was about to flake away into nothingness.

Without saying a word, he led the mercenaries up toward the peak. Maybe, just maybe, Rick Eilerman was on to something.

He wasn't counting on it, though.

CHAPTER 14

The steep climb to the peak was hell on Healy's knees. By the time they reached the top, they felt as though they were about to burst out of their sockets. He did his best to mask the pain and not show weakness, but with each passing minute, it proved more difficult.

The uphill journey took them another couple of hundred feet higher in elevation. Rick occasionally turned his head, just enough to see the others in his peripheral vision. He was grateful Atkins and his dogs strayed at the back. Ranch was a few meters to his right, with the others directly behind him.

The further they went up the hill, the less open space they had. The tree line stretched further out the higher they went, only leaving twelve feet or so of open space to walk along.

Ranch kept his eyes glued to the jungle. Behind that initial tree line was a maze of twisted shapes. Each one felt as though it could come alive at any moment.

His eyes panned up to a sparkly reflection between two trees. Weaved between them was the huge web from an orb weaver spider. He couldn't see the arachnid itself, but couldn't help but admire the artistry of its web design.

A batting sound filled his ears. The web exploded outward by a huge white mass. Ranch jumped back, startled by the huge albatross as it took to the sky. As he did, his foot hit a bump in the ground, causing him to fall backward. He sucked in a breath, pointing his shotgun high at the 'attacker'. It took a few moments for him to realize it was just a bird. The other men watched it fly off, then looked to Ranch. All at once, they chuckled at his expense.

"Comfortable?" Shaw asked. Ranch scowled at him, then stood up. His adrenaline settled, and he relaxed, allowing himself to chuckle at the moment.

That adrenaline returned with a vengeance as a world of birds burst from the jungle. They zipped between the group members, causing them to stagger out of formation.

"The hell's going on?" Ishmael asked.

"There's something in there," Rick said. The men took firing positions and aimed into the jungle. Birds continued soaring up and around, flying in unison toward the south end of the island. Away from danger.

Ranch watched along the Mossberg's iron sights, panning along the line of trees. He looked up where the web had been. A branch moved. It wasn't a swaying motion from birds brushing by. It was being weighed down by a mass. There was slight movement behind those thick green leaves. Whatever it was, it was no monkey. It had weight to it...the weight equal to a person.

"Up high," he alerted, aiming his shotgun high. He let off a deafening shot, pumped, and fired again. Smoking shells littered the grass. Pellets tore through leaves and bark. Several other team members blasted away. Bursts from submachine-gun and M4 Carbines ripped a hole in the tree line. They heard something cry out in a deep gravely roar. They caught glimpses of something falling from the branch. It hit the ground with a heavy *thud!* The group concentrated a few more shots where it landed, making damn sure that it was dead.

Rick pointed at Belville and Shaw, quietly instructing them to inspect the body. The rest of the group fanned out to provide cover.

Shaw slammed a fresh magazine into his M4 and moved in. Belville took the right, keeping a watchful eye on the spot where the target fell. He used his shotgun barrel to peel a branch to the side, giving him a clear view into the next few meters of jungle.

The tree leaves above dripped blood on the corpse that had perched upon it. The muscular recon specialist grabbed the corpse by the legs and pulled it out into the open.

"Fantastic," Zimmerman said. "We killed a jaguar."

There wasn't much left of its spotted brown fur coat to identify it. The shotgun and rifle blasts had torn the cat to shreds. Its white underside was completely soaked in red.

"Talk about a waste of ammo," Shaw remarked.

"Yeah, and if our presence wasn't known before, it definitely is now," Atkins said.

"Maybe *that's* what killed the sea lions," Ishmael suggested. "Look at the claws on that fucker."

Atkins studied the black curved nails protruding from the paws.

"It's possible. Don't know why'd they keep it in a crate. But it's possible."

"If that's what took down those big-ass things, then I'm glad we unloaded into it," Healy said.

Rick removed the partially spent magazine and replaced it with a full one.

"Let's keep moving," he said, resuming his march. "We're losing time."

Atkins looked away to keep his snickering expression from view. *Yeah, let's not waste time...while we sightsee along the coast.*

****

The southwest peak was like a crescent shape of landmass jutting out of the island to the northwest. It was made of solid rock, with hardly any vegetation in the forty yards between its tip and the tree line.

Rick stepped out to the edge of the peak and gazed out into the ocean, then turned and looked out toward the forest. Unfortunately, he couldn't see anything through the canopy. It was just one endless blanket of green stretching from one side of the island to the other. From what he could see, there was nothing to this place other than rock and grass. He unfolded the map again and studied the image. This spot was *not* here. There HAD to be a reason.

Atkins scowled openly at Rick.

"What now, *Sergeant?*" the mercenary leader said. "Gonna count how many birds there are?" Rick's face was buried in the map, his expression a puzzled one.

"I'm not sure yet." Rick regretted admitting that. As he expected, Atkins used it as ammunition against him.

"Alright, we need to push in. By the look of the sun's position, we've got less than five hours. Six at best."

"Not yet," Rick said.

"Sir, there's nothing here," Shaw said.

"There's something about this place," Rick reaffirmed.

"Only to you," Atkins said. "You're stalling."

"Shut up," Rick barked. He looked to the rest of the group. "Look around. See if you can find anything unusual. Any signs of industrial equipment. Weapons. Signs that anyone was here."

"This whole PLACE is unusual," Zimmerman said. The team fanned out with caution, combing through the grass and forest edge.

Atkins walked a hundred feet, keeping a yard of distance from the tree line. Nothing. His temper was nearing its boiling point. He peered into the jungle, rifle at shoulder height, seeing nothing but vegetation. No equipment. No movement, other than a few birds. Nothing.

He glanced back at the team, who were busy scouring the area for clues.

"What a waste of time. I can't believe we're actually doing this," he said. He marched over to Rick, who was examining the ground near the tip of the peak.

The former Sergeant recognized the thumps of angry footsteps. He stood up, his hands kept in an unthreatening position, though ready to be put to use should the mercenary get aggressive.

"I've about had it with you, Eilerman."

"Are we seriously doing this again?" Rick replied.

"Again and again, until you get your head straight," Atkins replied.

"It's *you* who needs to get your head straight. You're actually thinking this is just a simple manhunt? That there isn't more to this?"

"I know enough to take that threat of a time limit seriously," Atkins replied. He pointed back at the group. "Look around. It looks like they're on a goddamn Easter egg hunt. What next? You gonna have them paddle out into the ocean?"

The ocean...

Rick turned around and looked out into the water. The surface was a clear crystal blue. He could see the rocky bottom beneath the gentle swells. There were no signs of aquatic life he could see from this high up. He studied each formation, each one turning out to be some sort of rock.

There was one interesting detail: the seabed directly above him didn't shallow as the water approached the shore. Perhaps the rock wall continued straight down a few extra yards into the ocean? He got on his hands and knees and leaned over as far as he could to inspect the underside of the shelf.

"The hell are you doing now?" Atkins said.

"There's an opening down there," Rick said.

"What?"

"Down at the bottom. There's a cave entrance right below us."

Atkins leaned over to look. Already, his hands started to slip over the ledge. "Fuck!" he muttered. He tried again. He nearly had to get his entire upper half over the ledge before he could see it. It was a large open hole in the side of the island. The swells swept into it, with no sign of splashing any dead end.

"By the looks of it, it goes deep," Rick said.

"Yeah, it's a cave. Looks like a natural formation," Atkins replied. "It doesn't answer anything."

"You think it's a coincidence?"

"Maybe, maybe not. But there's no telling how far it goes into the island. Hell, it probably stops just beyond our field of view. Besides, there's no way to get down without breaking our necks. We don't have climbing equipment. Investigating it is a lost cause."

"There's a reason they didn't want us to find it," Rick said.

"There's no equipment down there. No sign that it was artificially built. Again, you're acting on a hunch."

"I'm putting the pieces together—shit!" The piece of ledge under Rick's palm broke off. Gravity began taking him with it. Rick felt himself starting to fall. A pair of hands grabbed his back and yanked him further back onto the cliff.

Several others hurried over, alerted by Rick's yell. He sat up, seeing Atkins standing over him.

"Thanks," he said, begrudgingly.

"Keep your thanks," Atkins said. "What you did was dumber than a doorknob. Your *investigation* as you call it, almost got you killed. All for what? So you could peek at a cave entrance?"

Rick stood up.

"I'm telling you, Angelo, there's a connection," he said.

"The connection you need to find is the one between your brain cells, because everything is all loose in there," Atkins said, pointing at Rick's forehead.

After a few moments of watching the altercation, Ranch decided to resume his patrol along the tree line. Most of the others were wasting time watching. He agreed with Rick's assessment that it was no coincidence that this location was hidden from the map. He needed to find the clue and help restore the group's faith in his sergeant.

He peered into the jungle, hoping to find anything out of the ordinary. Metal hatches. Footprints. Security cameras.

Nothing.

He started to turn away, only to notice a slight shift in one of the tree branches further along to his left. He walked a few yards down, shotgun poised. Probably just another stupid bird—he wasn't eager to be humiliated again. He took a single step into the jungle.

Streams of sunlight beamed down into the forest, giving the vegetation a golden appearance.

He saw rivers of red streaming down the trunk of a thick cedar tree. Ranch stared for a few seconds, making sure his imagination wasn't toying with him. It wasn't; he was looking at blood.

Ranch gazed up, following the stream where it originated from a branch ten feet high. Lying across it was a dead jaguar with flesh riddled with holes and tears.

The same jaguar the team recently shot a quarter mile back.

The creature waited, arms crossed over its chest, eyes unblinking, watching the human stumble into its trap. It has successfully separated him from the rest of the group. Furthermore, his attention was fixated on the diversion it had set up, leaving him oblivious to the black shape crouched between the ferns below.

The window of opportunity had opened. The creature sprang, arms outstretched, legs pedaling against the forest floor.

Ranch saw a blur of motion close in on him. Sharp claws punched six-inches into his abdomen. A huge mouth closed over his neck, sinking triangular serrated teeth into the flesh.

A brief scream escaped his throat before a river of blood drowned it out.

As the others reacted, the creature disappeared deep into the jungle with Ranch in tow.

CHAPTER 15

It moved like a fleeting ghost, its black figure barely glimpsed by the seven men. Had it not been for Ranch's yell, they would never have known he was gone.

"Christ alive!" Ishmael exclaimed. The brief splatter of blood acted like a curtain, further obscuring their view of the attacker. Jungle leaves swayed as Ranch was yanked into the jungle.

"Get 'em!" Atkins ordered. Shotgun blasts shredded the outer layer of jungle. Bits of vegetation exploded, then twirled to the ground. Zimmerman charged toward the tree line, letting off another couple of shotgun blasts, while Atkins and Shaw sent rifle rounds along the hostile's trajectory.

"Stop! Cease fire!" Rick shouted. Atkins continued blasting away, unloading half his magazine into the jungle. Rick grabbed him by the shoulder and yanked him back. "I said STOP!" His words sent spit into the mercenary's face. "You keep firing, you could hit Ranch."

"Enough with playing it safe, you dumb idiot! Look at *that!*" He pointed to the coating of blood dripping off the trees and shrubs. "He's dead already. And we just lost our chance to catch that guy on the run."

"Come on! Let's go after him!" Shaw shouted.

"No. NO!" Rick ordered. "I'm telling you, that's what he's counting on."

"Sir, it's got Ranch! You said yourself he might not be dead!"

"And now he's being used as bait. We have to hold back. Come up with a proper game plan."

"Yeah? Like walk around the island more? Get a suntan while we're at it?" Atkins said.

"Your fooling around is what got your marine killed," Zimmerman added. "If we keep listening to you, we're all dead meat."

"I see he makes a habit of leaving his men behind, doesn't he?" Ishmael remarked.

It took everything for Rick not to let his anger get the best of him. That struggle was shown with bulging veins in his neck and his arms tensing, ready to grab all three mercs and send them tumbling down the cliff.

Control. Control.

"Belville," Atkins shouted. The brawny tracker glanced in his direction, his shotgun still level toward the jungle. "You think you can track the feller down?"

"Piece of cake, sir. Anyone moving that fast, towing a human, is bound to leave signs that an amateur could pick up." He saw an expression of anger and betrayal in his former Sergeant's face. It hurt Belville to see it. He shook his head slightly. *Sorry man. But we have to do something.*

"Alright. You're on point. Ishmael, get behind him. Everyone else, on me," Atkins said.

Rick watched as his team got into position. They had *accepted* Atkins' leadership over his own.

"You son of a bitch, you're leading them right to it. We don't know what that is out there. If it's even human."

"Oh, here we go with this shit again," Atkins said. "Listen man, it's just some prick that's out there. Maybe he's been given a high dose of steroids or something, I don't care. He's not going to survive the next fifteen minutes. We've got a line on him, and we're going in. You can wait here if you want, pretend you're *Robinson Crusoe* for all I care. Count any sailboats that pass by. While you do that, the rest of us are gonna act like marines."

He turned and got behind Belville, who was carefully examining the area where Ranch was taken.

"There's a lot of blood," the tracker said. "There's a clear trail heading inland."

"Good. Let's get after it," Atkins said. He and Ishmael followed Belville into the jungle. Shaw and Healy went behind him, briefly glancing back at Rick. *Sorry man.* It was the complete opposite to what was expressed on Zimmerman's face. *Told you so, you dumb bastard.*

Rick watched his team disappear into the jungle, under the new lead of Angelo Atkins.

"Fuck," he muttered. He readied his rifle and followed his men into the island's interior.

CHAPTER 16

The jungle was a twisted mass of green and brown. Trees stretched for the sky, their branches in constant combat with their neighbors. Birds tore through the canopy, creating continuous movement above. Insects hopped from branch to branch in search of prey, while simultaneously on the lookout for predators.

Healy couldn't help but watch as a large beetle struggled in the white strands of the spider web it stumbled upon. The large arachnid appeared from the piece of bark it hid behind and watched as the clumsy insect snagged itself further. With long frolicking legs, the spider slowly moved out. Then like a bullet, it sprang and stung the helpless victim.

The pain in the medic's knees intensified. Initially, he agreed with Atkins' plan to go after Ranch's attacker. But now, seeing the maze of jungle all around him, he felt like the bug in the web.

Belville found another blood smear nearby on a large shrub. Next to it was a fern, crushed into the earth by the heel of a strangely shaped footprint. He studied the shape, instantly recognizing it from the beach.

"Something wrong, Bel?" Atkins asked.

"Nothing," Belville said. It was a lie. The sight of this print made it clear that they were unprepared for whatever they were up against. This was no human print, though it contained characteristics. It was too late to turn back, however. They were in the hornet's nest now, and they weren't getting out until they killed what waited inside.

He followed more signs at his two-o'clock. There were tree leaves resting on the soil. They were fresh, recently torn from place by a passing mass.

"This way," he whispered. He led them onward. Each tree was carefully examined before they passed it. Weapon muzzles and eyes panned together as though interconnected.

Still in the back of the group, Rick kept a watchful eye on their six. Each step had to be taken carefully, as it was easy to trip and fall in this place. Every time they stopped, neither foot was on even ground. He stared straight ahead, unable to see more than fifty feet beyond. At ten feet, his field of view was already compromised at any point. It was a crushing feeling, as if the jungle was closing in on him. And somehow, he suspected the one they pursued was well adept to hunting in this environment.

The front of the group moved on, while the center seemed to lag. Frustrated, Zimmerman stepped between Healy and Shaw, leaning in toward the medic Healy as he passed him.

"Listen, Doc. Keep up, or you'll find yourself on your own." Without waiting for a reply, he hustled ahead of them until he was right behind Atkins.

Rick quickened his pace to close the gap between him and the two marines.

"Healy? You alright?"

"I'll be fine, Sarge," the medic replied.

"You don't look fine."

"I'm good, Rick. I promise. I'll be good once we're through this," he said.

"We'll be done with this shortly," Shaw whispered. He spoke through gritted teeth. The desire for revenge was burning in his eyes. Those eyes scanned the jungle, desperate to catch a human shape. Even a glimpse. "That bastard can't be too far off."

Rick watched the wobbling of leaves after a gentle breeze cut through the island.

That's what I'm afraid of.

Healy took his mind off of his knees and quickened the pace to catch up with the others. Belville had stopped again. The mercenaries kept their weapons pointed outward, while he examined something on the ground.

"What's going on?" Atkins asked.

"He stopped here," Belville said. "Ranch's body was dropped here, then dragged all the way to—" he followed the trail to a misshapen trunk of a cedar tree. He checked the vegetation around it to make sure there were no surprises, then inspected a thin river of blood that trickled down from above. It streamed from a tall branch, down along the trunk, over the tumor-like growth coming out of the base, ultimately forming a small red puddle in the grass.

"Holy—"

There he was, strung over the branch. What was left of him, at least.

His arms were gone, as was his throat and any details of his face. It was definitely Ranch, though—that bald head couldn't be mistaken no matter how much the rest of him was mutilated.

There were claw marks all over the tree, leading up to the body.

"Jesus," Atkins said. "Bel, are there any more tracks?"

"I'm not seeing anything," Belville answered, searching around the tree. All there was were scratch marks all over the trunk. "It chose this tree, using the growth here as a boost," he pointed to the scratch marks along the top of the lump, "then took Ranch up there." He noticed how he was now referring to it as "it" and not "him."

"So, we're back to thinking it's an animal?" Zimmerman commented.

"Look at that. Nobody can make grooves like that."

"It probably dropped the body and a jaguar took it," Zimmerman said.

"Oh, give me a break," Shaw said. "Cats don't yank limbs off their victims."

"Oh, jeez," Zimmerman muttered. "Come on guys, we saw who grabbed your marine."

"It was practically behind the woods by the time we saw it."

"Stop with the 'it'. He had arms like a human. Ran off like a human—fact of the matter is that it was definitely a human. In black, no less. Probably stealth gear of some kind. But for the love of God, quit this notion that it was some monster."

"Keep it together, guys," Atkins ordered. With his weapon pointed high, he searched the tree. There was no movement other than a couple of birds. "Look alive. It's here somewhere."

"You're going with the 'it' too, huh?"

"Zimmerman, shut the flying fuck up. We can have this debate after we kill it," Atkins said.

"Bel, you sure it hasn't moved off?" Healy asked.

"There's no other tracks," Belville answered. "Either it's waiting up there, or it's using the trees to move around."

Atkins watched the trees, desperately trying to make out any humanoid shape. There was nothing. No black clothing. Claw marks stopped at a branch ten feet above Ranch's body. There was nothing up there but birds.

Birds…nothing was disturbing the wildlife. It probably wasn't in this tree any longer.

"Bel, keep searching for clues. Everyone, keep your eyes peeled. It's in the trees."

"It could be a diversion," Rick said.

"Bel said there's no other tracks," Atkins said. "It's here somewhere. Let's find it and kill it."

"Want us to fan out?" Ishmael asked.

"Not too far. Keep within sight of each other," Atkins said. "Bel, keep your eyes high in case it's up there."

"Got it."

The team branched out and searched the area of forest past the trail. Each man's breath was shaky as they nervously inspected every square foot of forest. Their eyes constantly panned up above them. Everywhere they searched, they carried that gut feeling that something was in the branches above them.

Rick followed Atkins to the northwest. His intent was to convince him to turn back. Before he could talk, he noticed that the mercenary had stopped and was sniffing the air. Rick could smell it too.

"Something's back there," Atkins said, pointing to the green landscape ahead of them. Plants stretched high from the dirt, nearly as tall as Belville. Combined with the low-hanging branches filled with leaves, they prevented any clear view.

Atkins whistled, drawing the others close.

"See something?" Shaw asked.

"Not sure," Atkins said. "Move up." They nudged themselves forward, taking it an inch at a time.

"Th—" Ishmael had to keep himself from shouting. He lowered himself down into a firing position. "There's something…thirty meters directly in front of me."

Atkins and Shaw, both crouched, gradually moved closer. Then they saw the black shape. It was no jaguar, that was for sure. Whatever it was, it had a bit of bulk to it. They could only see its back sticking out from behind a tree, ten feet high or so.

"Is that it?" Shaw whispered.

"Can't get a good look at it," Zimmerman said. He nudged himself closer, then found a spot where he could see the foot of the tree. There was no mistaking the blood smeared along the bark. The thing shifted, the top of its head bulging back and forth.

"Christ," he said. He waved Atkins over, allowing him the one square-foot of space that allowed direct view. The mercenary aimed with his M4, placed the back of the thing's head in his crosshairs, then squeezed the trigger. He watched the back of the skull pop like a balloon, splattering blood and brain into the woods behind it.

"Bullseye," he said.

"Careful, you don't know if it's dead," Rick warned.

"Well, I won't know unless I find out," Atkins said. He glanced at the others. "Ishmael, you're with me. Everyone, keep an eye out, just to help the Sarge feel comforted."

He rose from his crouched position and moved in, with Ishmael following close behind.

After twenty feet, he saw Ranch's severed arm at the foot of the tree. White bone stuck out of the end, broken off right where it would've attached at the socket.

Fucking bastard must've been having himself a little snack.

"Careful, boss. It's still clinging to the tree," Ishmael said. Heeding his advice, Atkins paused and studied the thing. He could still only see part of it from around the trunk, but it was definitely slung over, dead. Tired of dedicating time to caution, he sprinted the final ten or so strides, circled around the tree, and raised his muzzle.

Ishmael joined, his wild expression now a flabbergasted one.

"What the fuck...a fucking sea lion?"

It was a young male, only two-thirds the size of the ones they found on the beach. There were claw marks on its body, though it hadn't been torn up nearly as bad as the others. Rivers of blood ran from the bullet wound in its head, all the way to its flippers.

"How did it get..." Atkin's voice trailed off, seeing the pointed tip of a thin branch protruding out its back like a spike. He looked over his shoulder, seeing a bush that wasn't a bush... it was the rest of that branch. It had been cut away, the stump sharpened...all for this seal to be impaled upon it, while still alive. He looked back at the others and shouted, "Eyes up. It's another diversion."

The words made Belville's heart pump adrenaline. He immediately looked back up to the tree, ready to see the attacker emerge from hiding. Nothing.

It's got to be up there. There's nowhere else it could've gone—

The tumor-like growth shifted away from the tree and stood up. Razor-tipped hands, matching the color of the bark, reached out and grabbed him by the throat. Belville convulsed uncontrollably, the shotgun falling from his grip, while spiny fingers plunged deep into his neck.

"There's nothing here," Rick said. "Bel? You see anything? Bel?" He glanced back. Shaw, Zimmerman, and Healy looked too.

"JESUS!" the medic said. The other mercs immediately regrouped, and all at once, the team saw the huge thing. It stood six-inches taller than Belville, whom it had lifted off the ground. Its rigid exterior quickly faded from its bark color back to its natural dark-grey. Its mouth, void of cheeks or any other human features, gaped wide, bringing all its pointed teeth into view.

Blood spilled freely from Belville's twitching body. The creature twisted and ripped both claws along his neck, resulting in a sharp crack. The body fell free and hit the ground, while the head remained in its grip.

As quickly as they saw it, it darted into the forest. Rifle and shotgun shots struck the trees in its path.

"What the hell is that?!" Zimmerman yelled.

"Don't fucking know, but we're going after it!" Atkins said. "Hurry up! Let's go!"

"Didn't you see it?" Rick said. "It can camouflage! It hid right in plain sight!"

"That's why we need to chase it before it sets another trap!" Atkins said. He led the charge, hopping over Belville's headless corpse, then looked back before he was out of sight. "Come on! Move! Let's go!"

With no time to argue, the team stormed the jungle.

Already, there was no sign of the thing.

CHAPTER 17

Running feet pounded the earth like drums. Animals scattered as the stampede of bipedal creatures raced into the center of the island. Monkeys screamed down, while birds flew back and forth. Lizards scurried into their dens, while venomous snakes poised into striking positions.

Atkins led the team through barricades of shrubs and orchids. After several minutes of pursuit—at least, he believed it was pursuit, as there was no sight of the thing that killed Belville—he stopped in his tracks, only because of the pissed-off looking snake that was poised right in front of him.

"Shit," he muttered. He was no snake expert, but he had no intention of wasting time to find out if the thing was venomous or not. He pointed his M4 and decapitated the creature. Its leathery body coiled and spasmed, squirting blood from the headless stump.

The mercenary's eyes went back up to the forest. The jungle seemed to stretch on forever, concealing the beast from view.

"Jesus, Angelo. We're in over our heads. We need to turn back," Rick said.

"You go back if you want to. The rest of us will keep going," Atkins said.

"It knows what it's doing," Rick said. "It's diverted our attention to get Belville. It tricked Ranch with the dead jaguar. It's intelligent. It knows what it's doing."

Atkins looked up and searched the trees. Now he was looking for anything even slightly out of the ordinary. Every bump and twisting shape became a suspect. His mind was still absorbing the fact that the thing had camouflaged so perfectly. He had actually been standing right next to it, and never knew it. Imitated the tree so well, even going as far as to mimic scratch marks. He found himself wondering what it could be imitating now? The plants? Bushes? A log? The ground itself? The whole forest felt like it was about to reach out and grab him at any moment.

Also, it was fast and agile, despite being over seven-feet tall. By the look of its bulk, it had to weigh close to three hundred pounds at least. Then there were those claws, like human fingers, but bony and razor sharp. And those teeth—there was no other way of describing it. Clearly like a shark, as was its mouth. It had decapitated Belville with little effort. Contrary to how the movies portrayed it, that was no easy feat. At least, not for a man.

"What do we do?" Ishmael asked.

"We can't stay in one spot. We have to keep going," Atkins said.

"We need to go back to the shore," Rick said. "We need to be in the open where it can't ambush us."

"It killed Ranch, and now Belville. Now it's gonna find out it fucked with the wrong group," Atkins said. He searched the ground for any tracks. Unfortunately, this area of ground was mossed over, with thick layers of grass covering the soil, leaving no clear trail that anyone short of Belville's skill would notice. He couldn't keep the team in one place either, or else the thing would have more time to set up another trap. He picked a spot and continued on. "This way."

Rick clenched his jaw, then followed with the others behind him. Winding through the forest, each team member made a conscious effort to keep their distance from any tree or large bush.

Atkins led them through another hundred yards of jungle, then stopped. Something moved up ahead. He heard animals scatter. It was up ahead somewhere.

"Look alive," he said, quickening his pace. The team charged several meters, then stopped as soon as the rotting tree came into view. It had fallen years ago and was in various stages of decomposition. Broken branches were everywhere, some large enough to be tree trunks themselves.

The first one to catch the group's eye was a large fragment that stood straight up, having been staked to the ground from the crash. Atkins pointed his M4 and sent several rounds into it. Bits of bark exploded from the mass.

"Fuck this thing," he growled. He turned and saw a large log on the ground, just a few feet from the trunk. He fired a volley into it, then scanned the trunk for any bizarre shapes. "It led us here on purpose.

Thinks it can play games with us." He placed several rounds along the length of the tree, then into the graveyard of rotting branches.

The team started to fan around the base of the tree. As they did, Shaw wandered close to a nearby bush. He saw the edge of a log propped up behind it, its 'head' crested like the thing that killed Belville. He spun on his heel and fired several rounds into it, shrieking in terror. Bits of bark flew off the thing, and the driving force caused it to roll off the dead brush it had fallen on.

Ishmael and Healy rushed in to join the fray, only to see what Shaw had already discovered.

"Jesus," the medic whispered.

Fluttering wings drew his attention to the left. He watched several birds ascend into the air, some taking flight over their heads. As he watched them take flight, he noticed something arching through the air like a softball. In the split second he saw it, he assumed it to be one of the birds. It seemed to have wings. Then it started falling in a perfect angle, and he realized those 'wings' were eight flailing legs.

The thing landed square in the middle of his chest. Legs batted his vest, quickly finding something to cling on. Healy looked down, immediately recognizing the black eyes and hairy pedipalps of a very agitated Brazilian Wandering Spider.

He screamed and staggered backward, arching his back as if somehow that would put him out of reach of those hideous fangs.

"Get it off! Get it off!"

"Healy! Hold still!" Rick said. The panicking medic dropped his submachine gun and raised his hands to swat the arachnid, only to hold back from fear it would cling on to his hand and get his soft flesh. It scurried up to his collar, its forelegs touching his Adam's apple.

"Good Christ," Ishmael said. He saw movement in the corner of his eye, then the piercing pain of sharp hands clawing into his left shoulder. All of a sudden, he was yanked backward into the canopy and easily wrestled to the ground.

The beast fell on him, baring its teeth over a crested snout. Ishmael tried to scream, but instead convulsed from excruciating pain as the mouth closed down over his neck. A bony hand pressed down on his submachine gun, preventing him from firing it off. Warm blood filled its mouth, and the creature yanked its head back. Ishmael stared wide-eyed, seeing his own trachea and esophagus clenched in the creature's jaws.

It swallowed and proceeded to ravage him further.

"Hold-fucking-still!" Rick said. He grabbed Healy by the shoulders and slapped him across the chin. The edge of his hand caught the arachnid, knocking it several feet away. Atkins sprinted to the thing and stomped his heel on it.

"Fuck!"

Healy continued whacking his vest, slowly catching his breath.

"It's here! It threw it!" The words shot rapidly from his mouth. He looked into the jungle where he saw the birds fly out. "From there! It's in there somewhere."

"Could be anywhere at this poi—" Atkins looked around, "Ishmael?" The other four group members looked around, realizing the mercenary was not among them.

"Where the hell is he?" Zimmerman said.

"Ishmael?!" Atkins called out. He looked behind the fallen tree with no results, then turned back and saw Rick pointing at some skid marks on the ground. They went back behind a thick set of shrubs, definitely the result of someone being dragged back against his will.

The men formed positions near the shrubs, as though they were about to breach a door. All at once, they shot into the trail. Fifteen feet in was Ishmael's body, his throat and eyes gone, his ribs opened up, his submachine gun broken. Bloody footprints led straight ahead behind a line of trees.

Atkins fired several bursts into the jungle. "Son of a bitch coward! Show yourself!"

Rick and Zimmerman hurried next to him, ready to join the fray. The Sergeant stopped, his mind flashing back to the spider, the dead sea lion, the panther. He glanced at the bloody footsteps, laid out in plain view.

"Wait…" he turned around. Healy was right behind him, with Shaw just a few steps back. Suddenly, the jungle came alive, and a green, crustacean shape sprang out from the vegetation. Shaw screamed at the tooth-lined mouth and managed to fire a burst of rounds as the clawed hands grabbed him by the vest. Like a transient spirit, it dragged his flailing body deep into the jungle.

"There!" Rick yelled. He sprinted into the jungle after them. Already, the beast was out of sight. He heard Shaw scream from far within. Following the noise, he switched the M4 to full auto, and ran as fast as he could.

Shaw flailed his arms, unable to fight the much stronger thing off of him. He could feel its claws sinking deep into his ribcage. His feet were off the ground, the jungle slashing him as he was carried far off. It had knocked his M4 from his grasp when it attacked, leaving him with his sidearm.

Suddenly, the running motion stopped, and Shaw was suddenly upright, shoved against the side of a tree. The impact blew the air from his lungs. Still, he remained upright. The thing advanced, arms outstretched. It had reverted back to its dark grey color.

He yelled as the beast closed in on him and lowered its jaws to bite. He threw his left arm high over his face, then cried out as those teeth plunged deep into his forearm. Pain surged through his body as teeth ripped and bones were snapped.

His right hand still free, Shaw drew his Beretta and fired from the hip. Bullets smashed into the creature's abdomen and ricocheted. That's when he realized the creature's 'skin' was covered with an exoskeleton. He was being torn apart by a human crustacean…with the mouth of a shark.

The creature pulled its head back. Strands of flesh ripped away, and Shaw was forced to watch his own forearm separate from his elbow. Blood jetted from his stub like water from a broken pipe. He hyperventilated, his vision blurring from shock. As he slid down against the tree, the monster raised its left arm, fingers extended out like daggers.

It plunged them through his eye sockets and pushed the tips deep into Shaw's brain. It spat the severed arm out, then snarled at the dying commando.

Rick heard the gunshots. He was close. As he kept moving, he could hear the sound of a struggle.

He leapt through a line of bushes, then saw the creature holding his teammate back against a tree. Shaw's body spasmed, the fingers pressed all the way through his eyes. The creature turned and gazed at the former Sergeant.

A hundred questions raced through Rick's head in a single moment. What was he looking at? How could such a thing exist? Why did it exist?

It stood like a man, but there was nothing human about it besides its two arms and legs, and the proportion of its body. There were gills on its neck, the fleshy interior contrasting with the rock-hard shell. Its mouth was enormous and lined with razor-sharp teeth. A few inches above were two soulless eyes, staring right into Rick. He was looking at a shark that stood like a man—a Man-Shark!

Rick wasted no more time questioning what he was looking at. He pointed the gun and unleashed a volley of bullets that crashed along the creature's shell. It yanked its hand from Shaw's face, the limp body dropping to the ground. Bullets struck its neck and torso, the impact forcing it to stagger backward.

Rick ejected his empty magazine and reloaded the next one. The creature had started advancing, letting out a shrieking roar from its open mouth. He hit it again. This time, it did not back away. The bullets slowed its advance, but failed to penetrate its thick shell. It leaned forward, a moment away from sprinting.

In that moment, a flood of thoughts and plans raced through Rick's mind like a montage. He couldn't outrun it, outmuscle it, or hell, even shoot it. Grenades would take a few seconds to detonate unless…

He looked over at Shaw's corpse…and the grenades hanging from his chest. Rick aimed his rifle and fired. Several rounds struck the shell, breaking it open, allowing for another round to enter the breach and detonate the charge.

The creature was pushed to its right by the concussion, while simultaneously pelted by razor-sharp shrapnel. It let out a roar as one of the pieces found its way through the fibrous chitin in its left elbow joint.

Momentarily blinded by the pain, it failed to notice another grenade rolling near its feet, this one tossed by the human. The blast knocked it on its back, causing a small breach in its midsection.

The rest of the group emerged from the jungle and immediately began discharging their weapons at the thing. It leapt to its feet and darted into the forest.

The team ran after it, hearing its frenzied footsteps. After a few hundred feet, there was nothing but silence. Rick stopped and raised a fist, signaling the others to halt.

"We lost it," he said.

"We hurt it. This might be our chance. Shouldn't we keep going?" Zimmerman asked. Rick was surprised to know the former SAS commando was asking him instead of Atkins. Gone was the competitive and antagonizing attitude.

"I want to, but since we don't know where it is, we're more likely to stumble into another trap. Let's go back to the fallen tree. It's an open enough area for us to come up with a plan."

They caught their breath, then slowly backed up. Not one of them dared to blink. Their eyes were fixed on the jungle around them, searching for the strange humanoid creature inside.

It was wounded now. And a wounded beast was the most dangerous kind.

CHAPTER 18

Rick Eilerman unfolded the map and ran his finger along the southwest shore until he found the cliffs.

"Alright. We found that cave here, which is where the thing killed Ranch," he said, pointing a quarter mile from the marked cliff area. He traced his finger into the interior of the island. "We chased it roughly a quarter-mile inland, hooked south a bit before it attacked us. We continued east for a while then turned north, which puts us roughly around here." His finger settled at a point three quarters of a mile inland from the southwest corner.

Healy brushed the side of the fallen tree, making sure there weren't any arachnoid surprises, then took a much-needed rest.

"So, what now?"

"Staying here won't work," Atkins said.

"No shit. Our group's been cut in half," Zimmerman said. "I say we go back and inspect that cave Eilerman found. You said they erased it off the map. Clearly, they were hiding something. Maybe it's a way off this island."

"I'm all for checking it out, but the problem is we don't have a way to climb down the cliff," Rick said.

"I see. Well, I'm not fond of staying here. Who knows when that thing will come back," Zimmerman said.

"If it's not already here, watching," Healy added. Rick continued studying the map, then sighed.

"There's no good options," he said. "We're already in the middle of the damn island. No matter where we go, we'll have to trek through that jungle. We can head southwest to the cliffs again, but unfortunately, I think it's a dead end."

"What about that crate we found before?" Atkins said. "You said before it looked as though the platform went further underground. Maybe there's something to that."

"There was definitely some sort of construction here at some point," Healy said. "Though it may have been a very long time ago."

"That crate was definitely not carried through the jungle by some crane, and by the look of the canopy, it wasn't lowered by helicopter," Atkins said.

"Are you suggesting we head toward that?" Rick said. Atkins shrugged his shoulders, clearly frustrated and, in a rare display, overwhelmed.

"I don't know," the mercenary admitted. "I didn't expect we'd be fighting some…man-shark hybrid with armored skin."

"That can blend in with its surroundings perfectly," Zimmerman added.

"Hell, when I heard genetic engineering, I was thinking *Captain America* shit," Atkins said. "Figured a bullet would still solve that issue."

"Angelo," Rick stood up, realizing the mercenary was feeling guilt for the loss of their former teammates. Atkins had served with them too. Ate with them. Bled with them. And had to watch as they were slaughtered one-by-one in less than an hour. "Nobody would've been prepared for this. Hell, *SEAL Team Six* wouldn't have been prepared for this even if they had proper intel. This is something brand new, and we're the lab rats brought in to test it. You know what lab rats do when they get loose?"

Atkins looked back at him. "They bite back."

"Damn straight," Rick replied.

"I like the idea, but how do we 'bite back' exactly?" Healy said. "Bullets can't hurt it. Hell, it took a grenade and didn't die."

"It can be hurt," Rick said. "There's weak points in the joints where the shell can be penetrated. Plus, I think the grenades might have caused some damage, though it's hard to say. It ran off in the blink of an eye."

"The inside of its mouth is probably vulnerable," Atkins said.

"That, and the eyes," Rick said.

"Doesn't really inspire confidence," Zimmerman said. "We're talking about precise shots on something that can camouflage, move faster than something half its size, and can rip a person to shreds in an instant."

"Not to mention it's smart," Healy said. "That spider…it KNEW what it was, and that *I* knew what it was. Had that thing bitten me, I'd be dead in fifteen minutes at best. That, along with the fact that it knows how to divert our attention, tells us we're not dealing with some mindless animal."

Zimmerman let out an exasperated sigh. "If only we had a damn flamethrower."

"I'd burn this whole place down," Atkins muttered. "So, what's the plan, Sarge?"

"We're stuck with two options: head out to the coast where we're not surrounded by jungle, and hopefully lure it into a trap if it chooses to attack—which'll certainly lead us past the deadline. Or, we could continue hunting in this jungle—which hasn't worked out well so far, to say the least. Neither option ends well for us in the long run, so I think we need to search for answers."

"Check that crate again?"

"No," Rick replied, watching the map. "We'll check here." He turned it and pointed at what appeared to be an elevated region a half mile to the east.

"So, it's a hill," Atkins said. He shrugged his shoulders. *So what?*

"When I was on the west peak, I was able to get a look out into the island. There's no high elevation on the island interior, at least, not as significant as what's shown here." Atkins took the map and examined it.

"You think they're hiding something here?"

"They're hiding *something*, we know that for sure," Rick said.

"So, if that section of the map is obstructed, then why give us a map at all? Just to fuck with us? Drive us insane while their pet kills us?" Zimmerman said.

"I don't think they expected us to last long enough to notice the irregularities," Rick said. "Everything else on the map is accurate. I do believe this is a test, and that they were trying to present a genuine challenge for this thing. They just didn't want us heading to these precise locations."

"Any thoughts on what we'll find?" Healy asked. Rick stood up and double-checked his magazine count. He had taken the ammo from Shaw's, and gave his spare submachine gun to Zimmerman.

"Answers," he said.

CHAPTER 19

There was no sign of the creature. In the eyes of the team, that was almost as bad as having it staring them in the face. It was a fight to not fixate on every tiny movement in the jungle around them—and there were tons of movement.

They continued east toward the anomaly in the map in two-by-two standard formation, each person watching their side. The previous encounters left a certain level of paranoia in the group. In more than a few instances, they came across a strange shape in the jungle that they didn't trust to merely be a dead tree or a rock. A few shotgun blasts were wasted on these supposed apparitions, only to discover they were the real thing. They weren't worried about giving away their positions to the beast, wherever it was. It was clear that it was tracking them from the very beginning, and didn't need loud noises to pinpoint their location.

Atkins sniffed again. There was another foul smell in the air. Like before, it was the smell of death, only this one was more putrid than the others. Rick could smell it too. It smelled of decay. They watched the jungle, fearing it was an attempt to divert their attention.

"Stay together," Rick whispered to the others. "There's something up ahead." Zimmerman and Healy stood back-to-back, their guns ready to unload on any piece of jungle that looked like it would reach out at them.

Rick moved first, half-crouched and ready to sprint at a moment's notice. Checking his surroundings, he ascertained that the source of the smell was coming from behind a tree up ahead. He glanced back at Atkins, who nodded, signaling he had the Sergeant covered. Rick made the move, bolting around the tree.

Lizards and birds scattered, leaving a decomposing human corpse lying in the dirt. Rick observed the area for another few seconds, then waved the others over.

The four men gathered around the body. The midsection had been torn open completely, the entrails scattered around it. The insides were dark and shrunken, having been subject to exposure in hundred-degree heat and picked at non-stop by insects and lizards.

"He's been dead for...maybe four days," Healy said.

"He's definitely had a run-in with our pal," Atkins said, pointing at the slash marks on the throat. He gazed at the blood-stained white shirt and grey trousers. "They didn't give this guy any gear."

"No. They didn't," Rick acknowledged.

"Maybe they had to handle a disgruntled employee?" Zimmerman suggested. His half-joke failed to amuse.

"There are bite marks," Rick said. "They made a meal of him."

"They didn't arm him," Healy said.

"He wasn't meant to present a challenge," Rick said. "He was that thing's first kill. They gave it a taste for blood. We're the second phase: put it up against an armed squad."

"Not just any squad—Us," Atkins said. "Makes me wonder—" he knelt down by the body and checked the pockets. Whoever brought him here didn't bother to strip him of his belongings. Atkins pulled out the man's wallet and examined the ID inside. "Steven Benelli. No shit."

"You know that name?" Rick asked.

"Once I started my business, I got to know a few people in the Central Intelligence Agency," Atkins said. "A bonus of learning that side of the business was I got to learn how a few of our old operations got set up, and by who."

"Wait, this guy was C.I.A.?" Healy said.

"Retired, if memory serves," Atkins said.

"So, wait a sec; they brought in a *retired* C.I.A. operative to serve as a munchie for that thing out there?" Zimmerman said. "Wouldn't someone a little less-profile be more suitable?"

"I think there's more to it than that," Rick said. "Angelo, did you learn of any special operations connecting this guy with us?"

Atkins nodded, staring blankly at the corpse.

"Yemen. 2016. The water reservoir near Haraz during the Second Battle of Mukalla."

"Wait, the raid on the lab?" Healy said. "This is the guy who set that up?"

Rick nodded. "And he's the one they brought in first." Suddenly, it was all coming together.

Zimmerman shook his head. "Who the hell did you guys piss off?"

"We had gotten reports of chemical weapons being used during the Battle of Aden, which led to investigations into the black market. The C.I.A. uncovered reports of experimental testing, then found out that there was an American contractor in the area, who was getting funding from terrorist organizations trying to seize control of that area."

"Dr. Rex Berente," Rick said. "He formerly worked for the U.S. government. It isn't known what the hell they were trying to make him do, but it was no secret that he was a bio-engineer."

"Turns out the guy liked doing all kinds of sick experiments," Healy said.

"What kind of experimentation?" Zimmerman was almost afraid to ask.

"Biological. Chemical. Genetic. Sound familiar?" Atkins said.

Zimmerman nodded. "Let me guess. This dead agent uncovers the location, a plan was organized, and your fireteam was the one sent in."

"That's the gist of it," Atkins said.

"So, there's an ulterior motive than just testing a specimen," Zimmerman said. "This is revenge. You raided the guy's lab, probably destroyed a lot of research in the process, and now he's out for revenge."

"But…that can't be," Rick said. "I was right there. Danny and I fought our way to the lower levels. We found the lab and identified Dr. Berente. I placed a round between the eyes. I saw his skull open up. There was NO WAY he could've possibly survived that."

His mind replayed the incident. He remembered the scorching heat, the insurgents fighting to keep control of the outer perimeter. As they fought to eliminate all hostiles around the building, they had received word that Al-Qaeda forces were rolling in artillery, which forced Rick and Danny Rhee to act quickly while Atkins and the others fended off the attack.

He remembered the beat of his boots against concrete steps. He remembered the odd smells of whatever Berente was working on beneath. At the bend of the stairwell, he had taken down two insurgents, and Danny eliminated a third that tried sneaking in through the doorway.

Dust was raining from the ceiling. The ground shook from distant explosions that were gradually getting nearer. Rick remembered every grain of dust that trickled past him as he entered the lab. He and Danny entered and immediately shot down the four insurgents inside.

The image of glass tubes containing twisted specimens was frozen in his mind. He didn't even know what he was looking at. There was no other way to describe them as anything other than twisted malformations of animals, whose genes had been spliced together. There were cadavers with mangled bodies of Al-Qaeda terrorists who, either willingly or unwillingly, were subject to Berente's experimentation.

After eliminating all hostiles, Rick gazed upon the scientist. The white coat was almost black at this point from all the burning dust. He remembered smelling smoke at that moment. The upper floors must've caught fire somehow. Then the building shook.

Atkins was screaming in the radio for him to move.

There was no time. Rick placed the doctor's forehead in his crosshairs and squeezed the trigger. He watched his brains splotch the wall behind him. With Danny providing cover, Rick moved in, photographed the body with the nametag in plain view, then went for the stairs.

There was another explosion, and the ceiling collapsed. He remembered walking in a cloud of dust, reaching for a best friend that wasn't behind him anymore.

The sound of Atkins' voice snapped Rick back to reality.

"...genetic experiments. The fact that *we* were selected...that they had this guy killed. Whether or not Berente is dead, there is a connection."

Rick's mind filled with new questions. Could that scientist he killed have been a double? Was it someone else? An assistant? No, then why wear the doctor's nametag? He certainly matched the photo he had seen of him.

Rick gazed at the sunrays to recoup his sense of direction, then turned east.

"Our destination's up ahead. Let's find some answers."

CHAPTER 20

Silver monitor light glowed against his rectangular lenses, giving Doctor Berente the appearance of a comic book villain. He leaned back in his chair and took a draw on his pipe, his unblinking eyes watching the four men carefully patrolling through the island. The events of the past couple of hours had lifted his spirits.

Grey tobacco smoke wafted from the doctor's lips, forming small mountains between him and the main monitor. He monitored the team's location through the monitor feeds. They were making a straight line toward Operations. He was impressed, rather than alarmed. He had underestimated the leader's attention to detail. He was a scientist, not a tactical strategist, and he didn't consider the fact that they would actually try to examine the entire island and match it to the map—much less find the two irregularities that the vast majority of people would miss.

In a way, he was grateful the chain of events led to this. It would give him great satisfaction to get a closer look at the ones he hated most.

Berente could hear his guest approach from behind. His reflection appeared on the monitor screen, towering over the doctor.

"Is there a problem, Mr. Kruse?" Berente said.

"They're going to find this place. You sure you want that?"

"It won't matter in the long run," Berente answered. "Let them come. Let them see who defeated them."

"This could go wrong," the merc said. "Where's your pet? Why isn't it finishing the job?"

"Have some respect. It's a *he*, not an *it*. Be considerate of our guest in the next room," Berente said. He turned to face the monitor on his left. He had been tracking the specimen since its last encounter with the group. Its current location was a dark one. There was almost zero light;

he was practically looking at a blank screen—the tunnels. But he could hear it, breathing, growling. Molting.

"Is it...*he*, alright?" Kruse asked.

"Just licking his wounds," Berente said. He reached for the control module between the two monitors, his fingers finding the instruments marked for the underground systems.

"What are you doing?"

"I'm allowing access through the passageways," Berente said.

"Wouldn't that lead him back into—?"

"That's the idea," Berente said. The man was shaking his head, doubting the doctor's decision.

"This is lunacy. Your investors will not be pleased about this. If those men find their way in here, they could ruin everything. And if you let them in, what's to stop them from getting in *here*?"

"They won't live that long," Berente said. "Anything they discover won't change anything. They won't survive the hour, anyway. I want them to come in. They've earned it, since they survived up to now. I would love for them to see who it was that brought them here."

Kruse scowled. The doctor was allowing his personal vendetta to cloud his judgement. Unfortunately, there was nothing the mercenary could do about it.

"And the security systems?"

"The backup systems are down. These men will likely bypass the initial lock. I want it just hard enough for them to make their way in without realizing the trap they're stumbling into."

"I want my men on standby, just in case," the man said. Berente rotated his chair, finally gazing up at Kruse's scaly face. The mercenary had his arms crossed as he glared at the screen. "They're gonna be looking for Mrs. Rhee. I told you we should've kept her off site."

"It was important that she see this," Berente replied. "We just have a little longer to wait. Besides, it'll be nice to have courtside view when *he* gets what's coming to him." The doctor rammed a finger into the screen, landing it on Rick Eilerman's chest.

He smiled, eagerly anticipating seeing his creation complete its task. He rested the pipe in his left hand, then tilted it slightly to see the initials. *R.B.* Beneath those letters were his fingertips, the flesh forever a light red color from third-degree burns. He remembered the pain, physical and mental, from that day. Some of it had never subsided. Sometimes, he forgot his pinky and ring finger were no-longer attached to his left hand. And the ligament damage to his elbow; he could barely extend that arm beyond a forty-five degree angle. Usually, it remained clutched at his side, like the claw of a prehistoric reptile. It was still usable, as was the three-fingered hand attached to it, but it served as a reminder for what drove him to complete his research.

"Bring Mrs. Rhee to me, please," he said to Kruse.

"Bring her here? Into Operations? I should probably be escorting her off the island," Kruse said

"No. I want her *here*," Berente insisted. "You have a problem with that?" Kruse sighed and watched the men on the screen.

"It's your show," he muttered. He turned around and found the door, then disappeared into the connecting corridor. Berente returned his eyes to the blank monitor. He could hear the creature moving. It had heard the barricades retract, allowing it access further into the passageways. He then turned his eyes back to the four survivors. They were getting close now. Very close.

"Come on in," he said, tapping his scarred fingertips together. "Come into my house and I'll reintroduce you to an old friend—"

CHAPTER 21

What little doubt remained that the map image was altered died out when the team saw the large clearing. It was as if a hundred-yard hole had been punched into the jungle. Trees had been cut away at the base, the smaller vegetation cleared out, though some were in the process of growing back. Though the opening would've been small, it definitely would've been seen on the map.

In the center of this clearing was a single structure made of thick concrete. It was a simple cube shape, slightly rectangular, with one steel door on the front wall. There was no fencing around it. No security measures. All they saw were a couple of cameras placed high in trees near the perimeter. Overall, it almost felt like walking into somebody's backyard.

"Looks like a bunker," Atkins said. "I bet that door leads down into some sort of compound or facility."

"How the hell did they build this thing out here?" Healy asked. "If that structure goes underground, it would probably be a project that would take years to build."

"Unless it was already there," Rick said. "There are installations everywhere, dating back to research projects during the Vietnam War. Hell, some go back all the way to World War One. If I had to venture a guess, I'd say that whoever's here obtained an abandoned facility. Probably bought it through backdoor channels."

"Speaking of backdoor, you guys know we're being watched, right?" Zimmerman said.

"Let them watch," Atkins replied. He moved first, checking the ground for any trip wires or explosives along the way. To his surprise, there was nothing. "You'd think they'd put some sort of defensive measures to protect this place."

"Secrecy," Rick said. "That's what they were relying most on. Either it's out of everyone's jurisdiction, or it's owned by some government who's sponsoring whoever's down there. Hard to know when we still don't know where the hell we are."

"Besides, what better security would you need if you have that thing out there killing anyone who sets foot on this island?" Healy said.

"Well, I don't know about you, but I'm sick of this place and I'm ready to leave," Zimmerman said. He moved past Rick and went straight for the doorway. No alarms sounded. It was nothing but a reinforced bunker with a three-inch thick steel door. On the side was an identification panel for authorized personnel to swipe an ID card or punch in a code.

"You think we'll run into security resistance down there?" Healy asked.

"You worried?"

"Hell no! I'd rather deal with mercenaries than that thing out there," Healy said. "Who knows. Maybe we'll find some pain medication."

Rick nodded. He had heard Healy's knees pop more than a few times during their trek through the island.

"You think you can get us in, Zimmerman?" Atkins said.

"Just give me a sec...just let me...ah-ha!" The former SAS operative was able to unscrew the corners of the panel with his knife. He twisted each one out, then wedged the outer section off. There was still something keeping it attached to the main unit, but he was still able to get it open wide enough to access the wiring. "Keep an eye out for that big bastard, would ya?"

"Already on it," Rick said.

Zimmerman carefully examined each wire, tracing each one's connection and purpose, while muttering the process to himself. "Alright, this bastard goes here, that one goes there..."

The men waited several minutes as he figured it out.

"Sometime this century would be nice," Atkins said.

"Just making sure I won't be triggering any countermeasures," Zimmerman replied. He used his knife to slice away the coverings, then proceeded to splice some wires. "Alright, standby."

The men took position in front of the door. Zimmerman completed the bypass, and the steel door slid behind the frame. Behind it was a deep dark stairway.

Rick activated his flashlight and approached. The entire slope was comprised of thick concrete. It descended for thirty feet before flattening out at what appeared to be a corridor.

"No elevator?" Atkins asked.

"Not here at least." Rick took the first ten steps, his rifle pointed down at the stairway's end. He saw a dome-shaped piece of black glass on the ceiling halfway down. Rotating camera. Whoever was here had to know they had broken in. But there were no alarms. Unless…

He focused on the corridor entrance, feeling that armed resistance could arrive any moment. If they were caught in the stairway, they'd practically be fish in a barrel. He signaled to the others to hold back, then proceeded to the bottom.

Rick cleared the final five steps in a single bound, then landed in a firing position. He saw an ordinary door in his way with a mechanical lock. He looked up at the others and pointed at Zimmerman, who quickly descended the stairs and joined him.

Like with the exterior panel, he removed the screws with his knife and pried it open to access the wiring underneath. Since the control was a similar design as the last, he was able to cross the correct wires faster.

Both men stepped back and aimed their weapons into the corridor. It was empty, leading to a dimly-lit chamber five meters down. There was no movement, though he couldn't get a clear view. In a way, it was almost worse than meeting a dozen security officers.

"Something wrong there, Sarge?" Zimmerman said.

"Doesn't this feel a little *too* easy to you?"

"A bit," Zimmerman said. The two men waited in silence. "Listen, it's your call, but I think we should proceed. Either we go in there, or continue to be stalked out here. We're pretty much stuck between a rock and a hard place. At least in there, we might find some answers."

"And maybe find out where they're holding Ashley," Rick added. He waved Atkins and Healy down, then proceeded into the corridor.

Halfway down, Rick raised his left hand and silently counted down with his fingers. After reaching *zero*, the team charged down the second half and burst into the room. They split up in half, each duo taking a side of the lab. Flashlights panned around the area, finding nothing but computer tables, glass vials, and other electronic equipment. No people.

"No party?" Zimmerman muttered, disappointed there were no mercenaries for him to extract vengeance on. Atkins found a light switch and flicked it on.

Overhead panels illuminated a chemical laboratory with three main supercomputers, processing equipment, storage tubes, and various equipment that none of the men recognized. Rick walked into the center of the lab, gazing at the large computer console to his left. He felt he was looking at space-age equipment. Each console had at least two monitors, each one a different size and shape. They were powered down at the moment, making him wonder what purpose they served.

His eyes went to the large tubes on the left wall. Each one was a meter tall, containing some form of liquid chemical. Going by the colors, they contained a different fluid. Each one let out a mechanical hum. He touched the glass and was surprised to see that it was hot. He withdrew his hand, then continued studying the mechanism. There were pipes running up the walls and along the ceiling, connecting the various pieces of machinery.

"What the hell were they doing here?" Zimmerman muttered, looking at a large cylinder-shaped piece of equipment. Rick followed the pipes, which led to that very object. It was a processing unit of some kind. He glanced back at the tubes. Had they not encountered the creature out there, his first thought would've been chemical weapons. But he knew better. This was something else, probably genetic splicing. Or something else. He couldn't say for sure; he was no scientist, let alone a bio-chemist.

"Making monsters," Atkins replied. "You recognize any of this stuff, doc?" He looked over his shoulder and saw Healy in the back corner of the room, hovering over one of the consoles. Laid out on a flat desk extension was a layout of the anatomy of a starfish, printed out like a building blueprint. Next to it was a spiral notebook. He flipped it open, finding pages upon pages of text detailing the animal's cellular structure.

Atkins looked down at the image and scowled.

"Starfish? What use could that bring?"

"Whoever works here was, or is, trying to break down the genetic code. I'm sure you know how a starfish can regenerate its limbs."

"And how the other limb would become a whole new animal," Atkins added.

"Be a much cheaper way of creating a genetic hybrid once you have the first one," Healy said. He peeled the paper back, and found a similar anatomy layout, this time for a cuttlefish.

"I'm no scientist. What use would a squid bring to the table? They want to make a walking monster with eight arms?"

"Don't give them ideas," Healy said. "You saw how that thing could camouflage. They likely extracted genes from this species to allow the hybrid to blend in with its surroundings."

"I don't get it? What's the purpose of making such a thing?" Zimmerman said. "To make a weapon?"

"Yes," Rick said. "You saw what it did to the others. I'm just curious whether it's acting on free will or if it's being controlled somehow."

A tapping noise behind the back door put the group on alert. All weapons pointed toward it. Rick signaled Zimmerman to go first. They took breaching positions, then peered in through the glass panel. There was a small corridor leading to a few different sets of doors. He opened it and proceeded into the juncture, then heard the tapping again, this time coming from the closed door on the left. After taking breaching position, he peered into the small window on the upper half, seeing no obvious movement on the other side. There was nothing but a dark room. The door itself was unlocked.

Rick counted down from three, then kicked the door open. They swarmed the next room, but encountered no resistance. They heard the same tapping sound. Whatever it was, it was hitting glass.

Rick found the light switch and flicked it on, bringing what appeared to be a large aquarium into view. The room was huge, running for at least a couple of hundred feet in length, containing several glass tanks which held various creatures of all shapes and sizes. Sand sharks swam in tight circles, while hammerheads and whitetips overhead in a large twenty-by-twenty foot tank. Each creature was no larger than five feet—a stark contrast to what was in the adjacent tank.

"Jesus," Rick said, looking at the twelve-foot great white. Like the others, it swam in a tight circle. Its tank was equal in size to the other, giving it little space to swim. The grey-and-white fish looked sickly as it glided along the water. Its skin looked ragged and flaky, as though in the process of catching some type of disease. In addition, it looked underweight. The men actually found themselves feeling sorry for it.

"Wait," Atkins muttered. He walked up to the glass. "What the hell did they do to it?" Rick noticed the red dots around its body. Puncture wounds, some of which had not quite healed. It was as if the fish had been jabbed repeatedly with a sharp stick. Or a hypodermic needle.

"DNA samples," he said. He stepped away and observed the rest of the lab. There were cuttlefish, lobsters, crabs, starfish, numerous species of fish including deep water specimens, all biding their time within their glass prisons. The chirping of birds was the first indicator that it wasn't just sea life being stored here.

On the far end of the lab were various species of amphibians and reptiles. Exotic tree frogs hopped from one artificial branch to the other, while lizards stared aimlessly out into the lab like patients in a mental asylum. Venomous snakes slithered in different tanks, each mimicking a different environment. There were king cobras, black mambas, timber rattlesnakes, along with green anacondas, boa constrictors, and some pythons. Other aquariums displayed insects such as the praying mantis, several species of ants and beetles, several spiders and scorpions, and worms.

"I'd say they're getting a little too ambitious," Zimmerman said. He looked around the back of the lab. There were no doors or equipment other than filtration pipes. "Something tells me there's more to this lab than what we're seeing."

Atkins stepped back into the juncture. At the far end were a set of elevator doors. There was only a *down* button. He pressed it, then stepped back cautiously as the doors slid open.

"Well, if there is more...it's gonna be down there." The others returned to the juncture and looked at the elevator.

"We sure we want to go down there?" Healy asked.

"You can wait here if you want," Zimmerman said. He stepped in and rested his finger against the control panel. He glared at the others, who waited outside. "Coming?"

Rick hated the idea of potentially being trapped in this small five-by-five box. More worrisome than that was that they'd potentially be a shooting gallery for anyone waiting below. *Better than getting my throat torn out, I guess.* The three men stepped inside. Zimmerman pressed the button to the lower level, and watched the doors slide shut.

CHAPTER 22

The descent to the lower levels took less than five seconds. In that time, they felt the elevator zip down the tracks and stop at the next juncture. The doors slid open, taking them into another lab.

Immediately the smell hit them. It was a combination of rusted steel, chemicals, and something they could only describe as a rotten, fishy smell. The lights were on, as were the two computer consoles. Only half the lights were working, reflecting on grey surfaces. Most of the room appeared to be made of some kind of metal, with the exception of the back wall, which was made of some type of granite.

To the right was something that almost appeared to be an MRI machine, only standing straight up on end. It was cylinder-shaped, its front exterior serving as a thick metal door with a thin rectangular window. Rick peered inside. There was no occupant, but he could see several restraints and tubing within the limelight.

On the wall across from it were four large aquariums, the glass foggy, covered in algae, and poorly maintained. Each one was a different size, the largest resting on the bottom. It was roughly twelve feet in length. Behind that foggy glass was movement. There was something in it.

Atkins approached and cautiously pressed his face to the glass. On the other side was what appeared to be a small shark. It was swimming in circles, docile in appearance. As Atkins watched it, he noticed something odd about its shape. Suddenly, the creature attacked the glass. He jumped back and pointed his gun reactively. The shark tried biting at him, its nose bumping against the fogged barrier between them. That's when he noticed there were no teeth. Its mouth was a birdlike beak. Its skin was spiny and bumpy, its color an orange-white. Its eyes were solid black with no pupils, with strange tendrils protruding from its pointy snout. After a few seconds, it gave up and resumed its circular swim.

"Mother of Mary," he muttered, unable to take his eyes off the hybrid. He looked up at the top one, seeing another horrifying specimen. This one was a smaller shark, which was resting along the bottom. It was twitching its tail, clearly in an agonizing state. Two claw-like legs protruded from under its left pectoral fin, with nothing on the other side. It was a partial genetic reconstruction—a failed specimen, left to die in agony. God only knew what its insides looked like.

The next was an eel of some sort. It seemed normal—other than the fact that it had two heads. Its body had a sick, veiny appearance, and it was clear the two brains were fighting for dominance over which controlled the body.

The last one—he could barely look at it. Atkins was a man who'd shot more people than he could count, seen mass graves, torched buildings, seen civilians massacred—including their children. He'd seen more decaying bodies than the average coroner, yet, he could barely stand to look at what was in that tank.

It was practically a swimming set of jaws, with long needle-like teeth, with a squid mantle for a body. What really disturbed him were the tentacles; three of them had human hands at the tips, bony fingers reaching out and clawing at the water. They were uneven in size, each 'hand' containing a different number of fingers. One had two, another had five...but there was no mistaking the shape. They were human.

The mouth opened, exposing a red, fleshy tongue.

Atkins felt his stomach turn. He faced away from it, took a breath, and regained control.

Zimmerman took a seat at one of the consoles and started typing keys. There was the reflection of an active monitor on his face.

"You got it to work?" Atkins asked.

"Looks like they left it on," Zimmerman said. "I'm hoping I'll find something useful in here. Right now, all I'm seeing are data files for whatever creepy shit they were doing here."

"See if you can find a layout to this place," Rick said. "Everyone else, keep looking around."

At the back of the lab was a juncture. On the right was an entrance to another lab, and straight ahead was a steel door in the rock walls. Rick inspected the steel door. On its right side was a small panel with a set of buttons. He pressed a few to open it, only to see the LED reading *LOCKED.*

Interesting.

"Zimmerman? You think you can get a crack at this?" he said. Zimmerman got up from the computer and took a look at the panel. He studied the edges, checked the buttons, as well as the door itself.

"Can't do anything with this one," he said. "I can't get the panel off, and it's locked from the other side. And by the looks of it, there's no getting through that door without an explosive."

"Damn," Rick muttered. He turned to get a brief look into the next lab on the right. There was no human presence, nor was there sound other than that of dripping water and humming machinery.

They proceeded into the next lab…immediately stopping at the sight of a single flat table, covered in a glass dome. They saw IV-lines pumping fluids through a passage section into whatever it was it contained. It was throbbing, organic…alive.

"Fuck me…" Atkins muttered. He was gazing at a human arm. Humanoid, at this point, as it was human only in its basic shape. The outside was a rigid shell, which encompassed the fingers, giving them a pointed, claw-like tip. The shell was dark grey, bent slightly at the elbow, with IV lines feeding into it from the open back. The fingers curled slightly, grazing the metal surface they rested on.

There was fibrous growth along the back, with veiny flesh stretching out, slowly generating new flesh. They could see the pinkish growth of muscular tissue underneath the soft edges of the shell.

"Maybe this was a bad idea," Atkins muttered, staring at the thing. His eyes went to glass storage jars on the walls, each one containing embryonic specimens preserved in fluid. Some looked like curled shrimp with bulging human-like eyes, while others were more fish-like or reptilian.

Alongside the arm was a large electronic device with tubes feeding into the arm's open end.

"I think this is where the starfish genes play a role," the medic said. "This arm is growing into a whole new body."

"So, it's alive?" Atkins asked.

"Yes, but only because of the bypass machine. From the looks of it, it can regrow, but it needs to be kept alive in order to do it. They haven't perfected the gene sequence yet. Each piece that gets severed will die before it grows into a new animal."

"How fast do you think one of these things can regenerate on its own?"

"Something with its own heartbeat? I have no idea," Healy said. "A normal starfish takes months or even years. But I wouldn't be surprised if the guy running this lab has accelerated the process. Minutes? Hours? A couple of days? It might be different for each specimen."

Healy continued observing the lab. There was an open hallway on the righthand side leading to three basic rooms. There were no mechanical locks or any other security measures. He opened the one on the left, and saw what appeared to be an operating room. There was a single table in the center, with shackles located where human arms and legs would normally be. There was monitoring equipment and pipes running down the walls, feeding into huge cannisters.

The medic stepped inside, then stopped at the sight of a towering object on the left-hand side. It was like a big metal tomb, like the machine in the other lab. Green lights blinked, showing monitoring signs. There was a canister secured to the side with IV lines feeding from it. Healy leaned in for a closer look.

C_3H_3.

"Cyclopropane," he said to himself.

"What's that?"

Healy almost jumped. He hadn't heard Rick step up behind him.

"It's an anesthetic," he answered. "They were doing surgeries in here. Judging by those restraints, I would say their last patient was a person." There were several cannisters of the cyclopropane on standby. Either the doctors here had a lot of patients, or they needed a high dose of it. He continued examining the machine. It was on mechanical wheels. There were visible locking mechanisms on the door. "I think this was a secure way of transporting the patient. If I had to venture a guess, I'd say they were concerned with him getting a little rowdy."

"I imagine genetically altering somebody might be a little painful," Rick said. He looked up and around, noticing the pipes lining the walls. "Recognize all this?" They fed down from the ceiling, seemingly traveling up to the surface. Healy nodded. Those pipes were linked all the way back to that weird chemistry room above.

They backed out of the room and checked the others. They were basically the same, though the operating tables were calibrated for different organisms. It was clear the staff here were very busy in what they were developing.

Zimmerman shouted from the specimen room. "Hey, guys!" The three marines hustled back to him.

"Find something?" Atkins said.

"Found a file on our island," Zimmerman said.

"No shit. Where are we?"

"By the looks of it, it's some private island forty miles off the Coast of Colombia," Zimmerman said.

"Oh, lovely," Atkins said. "They're probably the ones funding this."

"There's more…" Zimmerman clicked a couple of buttons, then brought up an image of the island. It matched the image on their map, except this computer actually displayed the small peninsula near the cliffs. The mercenary tapped a button, and the satellite image turned blue with several red lines streaking through it. Rick studied the image, then realized they all originated from the cave he discovered. "That cave you found, Eilerman; by the looks of it, it branches off into a series of tunnels that runs through the entire island."

"What are these little squares?" Atkins asked, pointing to tiny markers in the lines. There were maybe a dozen or so of them, scattered along the map.

"Entry points. Hatches," Zimmerman said. "They're everywhere, probably to allow access into the cave from various point in the island. But the best part is this." He minimized the image and tapped a few keys. A new image came up, displaying a more detailed map of the facility and the interior. There were a series of corridors expanding from that locked door that fed into *Operations* and the living quarters. He scrolled the image to the southwest corner near the cave. "That cave you found, it's a fucking docking site. They've got boats there, hidden inside the cave."

"Son of a bitch," Atkins said.

"No wonder they left it off the map," Rick replied.

"But how do we get to it?" Healy asked. "We can't get through that door. And we don't have the equipment to climb down the cliff to get in the cave."

"There is a hatch near the cliff," Zimmerman said. "It's probably hidden in the jungle, which is why we didn't see it. We could head back to the surface and go back there."

"I'm not so fond of wandering the jungle any more than I have to," Healy said.

"What about the tunnels?" Atkins said. "Scroll back to the main facility. I thought I saw some of the tunnels linking to it."

"They're everywhere. Whether they're artificial or manmade, I have no idea," Zimmerman said. "There's a juncture, maybe a thousand feet, uh…" he pointed back to the connecting lab. "That way. There should be a passageway that'll lead us to the tunnel."

Atkins hustled back to the lab. "The electronic doors at the back?"

"Yes," Zimmerman answered.

Fuck! Atkins thought. The door was the same design as the one leading to *Operations.* He presumed it was locked on the other side as well. The other three men grouped behind him.

"Give it a try," Rick said. Atkins shrugged, then pressed the access button on the panel. To his surprise, the door slid open with an icy hiss. He stumbled back, surprised, and gazed into the empty corridor.

"Interesting," Rick said. "Either they simply left this unlocked, or they're deliberately trying to keep us from getting through that other door."

"You wanna hold back?" Atkins asked.

"I don't know. Something about this doesn't feel right," Rick replied. After a moment of thought, he took the first step in. "Let's proceed."

"What about Ashley?" Healy said.

"Let's just see if we can locate this thing first," Rick said. "If we can find a path to the dock, we'll double back and find a way through that door." The men nodded in agreement. "Alright. Everybody on me."

CHAPTER 23

The corridor was long and dull. Its floor was made of a metal tile that had rusted over the years. The only technology they saw were lights on the ceiling, and even some of those needed to be replaced. The fishy smell worsened the further they went.

Rick Eilerman felt like he was exploring the passageways of an abandoned ship. It was clear that portions of this facility had been poorly maintained, which made him wonder how many staff were stationed here. Whatever this place was, it had been built long ago, and was now repurposed into this lab for genetic splicing.

They heard water dripping somewhere further down.

"Zimmerman, you said it was only a thousand feet," Atkins mumbled.

"The computer didn't give me a precise distance. I was judging by the line," Zimmerman replied defensively. Atkins was getting nervous. There was only one logical reason the next section would be this far away from the rest of the lab, and that was to keep whatever was there isolated.

Rick's eyes went to the floor. There were scrape marks from something heavy, which was transported on wheels. He thought of the big machine in the operating room. It was obvious that the 'patient' was delivered to wherever this passageway ended. He tried to imagine the scientific process, but all it did was give him a migraine, not just from the complicated science, but from knowing that whoever underwent the procedure probably endured physical pain beyond the limits of the human psyche. Then there was the psychological factor of the body transforming. It made him wonder—that thing out there was part human, but how much of its humanity was still there? It was cunning in the sense that it could strategize an attack, but beyond that, did any human characteristics remain? Or was it all beast?

"Up ahead," Atkins whispered. "There's an opening." The team hugged the walls and gradually approached. There was no window on the barricade, leaving no way to see inside. Zimmerman activated the access panel. They heard the turning of gears, and the door opened.

A rush of moist air hit them. With it came the horrid stench of rotting bodies. Artificial light streamed down from above, keeping a high humidity level.

The chamber was large, resembling a biological exhibit intended for large reptiles. There were stone walls with large alcoves, covered in claw marks. Artificial trees stood high, their tops reaching the fifteen-foot ceiling. There were rocks and crevices, in addition to a small valley of fake grass. This whole chamber looked as though it was conditioning the creature to various environments.

In the center was a large pool, containing water filled with soot. It stank horribly, as though it was taken from a swamp and dumped there. There was a salty smell with it, which made their noses dry up despite the humidity.

Rick turned around and gazed up at the back wall. There were several cameras pointed down at the enclosure, stationed next to speakerphones. In the center was a sixty-five-inch monitor.

Somehow, I don't think that's for watching cable.

Zimmerman wandered into the tall grass. There was something several feet in, lying on the ground. The grass around it was caked with dried blood. He looked back at the others.

"Psst!" They slowly approached and followed him. Thin blades of grass folded under Zimmerman's feet as he ventured further into the artificial field. After wandering six feet in, he noticed large flaps, dark green in color, trailing brown, crusted blood. He took three more steps, then saw the elongated skull, connected to a twelve-foot mass.

"Shit," he muttered, backing up a step.

"What is it?" Atkins asked.

"A dead alligator," Zimmerman said. The others gathered and looked at the corpse, which was almost void of any flesh. It was a brownish-pink spine and ribcage, with only a few pieces of skull remaining.

"And there." Atkins pointed his finger a couple of yards past it. There was another corpse in the grass. Judging from the large nails and fangs, it was feline.

"It's a lion," Rick said. There were more skeletal remains discarded in the grass area. Almost all of them were predatory species that were known to have little fear. It was the first step in conditioning the hybrid to kill and fight for its life in close-quarters.

"Jesus," Rick muttered, thinking of the creature being locked in this underground prison, with no human interaction for God-knows how long. If any human element survived the operation, being trapped down here alone, forced to kill for its food, definitely finished the job.

"How'd they get this stuff down here?" Zimmerman asked.

"I can tell you," Atkins said. He was pointing at a steel segment in an alcove within the rock wall on the right. Centered at its base was an open elevator door. Healy glanced inside, seeing the steel tracks. There was no lower level, meaning the compartment was lifted straight up.

"Now we know where that storage container came from," he said.

"But no tunnel," Rick said.

"Zimmerman, I thought there was a way out!" Atkins barked, frustrated.

"It's supposed to be here!" Zimmerman defended. "Maybe there's another entrance?"

"Forget it," Rick said. "Let's double-back."

"We came here for answers, Eilerman," Atkins argued.

"We got them," Rick said. "This was where they kept the thing. They fed it live animals…DEADLY animals, teaching it to kill with its hands and teeth. There's nothing else we can learn from this. We came here to find the underground tunnel, but it's not here. Let's head back."

As he started for the door, a blaring sound filled the room.

"Fuck!" Zimmerman said.

After several seconds, the high-pitched blare settled, and a human voice took its place.

"It's a pity you want to leave. There was so much you were about to uncover."

The monitor flickered, them beamed a white light into the room. The monitor adjusted, and after a few moments, the men saw the face of a man in his fifties staring back at them. His brow was riddled with burn marks. He had little hair, as much of his scalp was mangled. He wore rectangular glasses, which reflected light of their own. It was clear he was watching them through a computer monitor.

"It's about time you had the balls to show your ugly face," Atkins said.

"Who the hell are you?" Rick asked.

"Dr. Berente," the figure replied, smiling. All eyes went to Rick. He was shaking his head, his face like that of an enraged demon.

"That's a lie. I put a hole through his skull. I saw him go down. I photographed his body. Dr. Berente is DEAD!"

"It's not a lie, though you are correct. Dr. Rex Berente is dead. I am Dr. *Wallace* Berente."

"Wallace?" Rick said, under his breath. His jaw was slack. It wasn't often that Rick Eilerman was speechless. There was so much he wanted to say, but couldn't get the words out.

"Oh shit," Atkins muttered. It all made sense what was happening now. Rick had successfully neutralized the target back in Yemen, but little did they, and probably the government, know that Rex Berente had a sibling.

"Let me guess," Zimmerman said. "Baby brother?"

"Big brother. Together, Rex and I were testing the limits of genetic engineering. We were developing new vaccines! New medicines! Better yet, we were working on developing the human body. To make it perfect. To heal itself without the need of outside influence. I was making the human race INVINCIBLE!"

"Yeah...this guy's all there," Healy muttered.

"Then you took everything away from me," Berente said. "My research. My lab. My *brother*."

"Yeah, I remember him," Rick said. "I remember he was building chemical agents and selling them for a hefty bounty. I remember seeing all the civilians your buyers killed with it. Faces mangled from acid burns. Bodies twisted and disfigured. The mental agony and transformation people underwent as they suffered. Was that part of your method for developing the human body?"

"Our research was not cheap. We had to pay for it somehow. The U.S. decided it needed to throw money around on building more guns and bombs, and government employees in branches that serve no purpose. We took our services elsewhere. Buyers wanted weapons, and weapons sell. Simple as that."

"So, why show your face now?" Atkins said. "Is this some comic book scheme of showing the enemy 'who it was that defeated them'?"

"In fact, that's *exactly* what I'm doing. I have no shame in admitting it. You see, it's personal to me," the doctor said. "I took the time and effort to track you down...with some help from my sponsor, of course. For years, I planned this moment. I knew my sponsors would want to test my creation with real trained soldiers, and today, I provided that for them. And today, I watched, one-by-one, as my creation slaughtered the very fireteam that killed my brother." The doctor gazed over at Zimmerman. "I do realize not all of you were responsible, and to you I apologize. Unfortunately, you were in the wrong place at the wrong time. And I can't afford loose ends."

"Loose ends, huh?" Rick said. "All that bullshit about hunting down a fugitive was just a means to get us in that jungle. We were *never* meant to get off this island alive."

"You're smart, Sergeant," Berente said.

"So, what about Ashley? You consider her a loose end too? Is she even alive?"

"Mrs. Rhee?! She's my most valuable asset. Haven't you wondered how we were able to track down most of you?"

Rick's eyes burned into Berente's face. His rifle shook in his hands. Not since his rookie days as a marine had his emotions threatened to get the better of him, but now, he felt like an atom bomb waiting to go off. *What did the doctor mean by that?* It was a question felt by the other three. Even Zimmerman, a man who had no emotional connection with Danny Rhee or his wife Ashley, was tensing up with anticipation.

"Where is she?" Rick said. The words came out just above a whisper. He was barely keeping it together…and Dr. Berente was loving it.

"She's here."

"WHERE?!" Rick exploded. He pointed his rifle at the screen, as though somehow that threatened Berente. The doctor watched the foolish emotional behavior and laughed, enraging Rick further. "Tell me where she is, or I'll put a goddamn bullet in every little specimen you have in this place."

"Eilerman," Atkins calmly said. "Stop." He put a hand on Rick's shoulder, edging him back from the monitor. Rick whipped around to look the merc in the face, then saw the relaxed demeanor. Atkins was breathing slowly, keeping his wits. Behind that demeanor was a man also close to snapping. But he'd already acted brash today, and wasn't going to do it again. Rick nodded, understanding the gesture. He was giving the enemy exactly what he wanted. It was going to stop now.

Rick inhaled deeply, then raised his eyes back to the screen.

"Where is she?"

Berente smiled, then stepped back from the screen.

"Right here with me."

First, they saw a shadow, then a human figure step into the frame. Ashley looked healthy and well. Almost *too* well. She was clean, her hair hanging back. She wore jeans and a scoop neck tank top. She stared into the camera, her face showing an odd mixture of contempt and satisfaction.

Rick couldn't help but notice her demeanor. She wasn't bound in any way. In fact, there were no obvious signs of struggle or abuse. There were no bruises, no wrist marks from handcuffs. Her face wasn't discolored. She didn't even look scared.

"Ashley..." he said. His first instinct was to ask if she was okay, but it was clear that wasn't the right question. *No...she couldn't have been involved in this. Berente was lying. Had to be. He'd managed to deceive everyone up until now, and why would Ashley do this to her friends? Her HUSBAND's friends!*

"Rick," she said, a half-greeting, half-bitter-acknowledgement. It was the polar opposite of the woman he'd spent the night with—the woman he'd known for ten years. Rick felt as though his insides were melting. His stomach swirled, his heart drumming hard. All of that paled to what his head felt like.

"Ashely?" Atkins said, speaking for his teammate. "Are you part of this?"

"I've been planning this all along," Ashley said. Her voice was cold as ice, equal to her stare. Had they been in the same room, Atkins would suspect she'd execute them herself, judging by that stare.

Rick felt like he needed to take a seat. He turned around, questioning whether it was real. After seeing his friends killed by the creature, he thought this day could not possibly get worse. He absorbed it and let it sink in.

"Don't act shocked, Rick," Ashley said. He whipped back around.

"Oh, pardon me," he snarled. "You're right. I should've known my late friend's wife was plotting to kill me and my old unit, with the help of a mad scientist!"

"You had it coming," Ashley said.

"Why?"

"Because you *left him!*"

"Left...Danny?" Rick said, his mind briefly flashing to the burning ceiling collapsing behind him. "I tried to get him out, but he was gone. We had to get to the extraction point. Danny's dead."

"No. He's *alive*," she said. Behind her, Berente was smiling, his crooked arm held close to his body. She looked over at him, then back at the team. "Danny was still alive when that building came down. You left him to die when you could've saved him. Danny would've died, but he didn't. Thanks to Dr. Wallace Berente."

"Stop believing his lies, Ashley," Rick said.

"What lies?" Berente stepped forward. "I was there. I opened the doors, and I heard the shot. One moment, my brother was standing there, unarmed, unthreatening. I watched your bullet cut through his skull."

Berente closed his eyes and remembered the event.

He remembered downloading data from the computers and gathering irreplaceable samples when he heard shots coming from the chem-lab. He called for Rex but had no reply. He remembered running down the corridor, stopping at the two double doors that led to the chem lab. He saw Rex, alone, his armed escort shot to oblivion. The bullet passed through his skull. Wallace Berente froze, unable to move. There, he watched the Marine Sergeant step over his brother's body, identify him, and snap a photo, before hurrying back to the stairwell.

He remembered the world shaking as a blast hit above, and suddenly the ceiling opened up. It was as though Hell had taken the place of Heaven, and had now decided to rain down on his world. He screamed from the scorching pain in his scalp, which snapped him out of his state of shock. He burst through the doors, the hot metal ravaging his left hand. Fire had already encompassed his dead brother. There was nothing Berente could do to save him.

More ceiling rained down, striking him left and right. Behind the explosions were the sounds of running feet. Security forces were approaching, yelling for him to come along.

Then he saw the debris shifting by the stairwell. There was someone underneath, burning alive. Against his sense of self-preservation, Berente approached the debris. It was one of the marines. Corporal Danny Rhee.

"I pulled him from the flames," Berente explained, holding up his mangled hand. "I still bear the mark of that day, but it was nothing compared to him. His skin was charred, with hardly a square-inch spared. His arm was completely shattered, his face and body disfigured. Any compassionate person would've put him out of his misery. Instead, I made him *better*."

Silence fell on the group as they took in what Berente was explaining to them. Healy went from being composed to trying not to vomit. That thing…that malformed monster…was not some random person. It was their friend, their brother-in-arms. It was Danny!

"He saved my husband's life, after you left him to die," Ashley said, her face a demonic scowl. "Now, you will pay for what you did to him."

"Christ, Ashley!" Rick said. "Don't you…haven't you *seen* him?! That's not Danny!"

"It is Danny!" she replied. "He would've died, otherwise. It was the only way." Rick stammered. Words couldn't describe his disgust. Not only was she *okay* about the hideous experiments performed on Danny, but she helped Berente track them down! All this time, during every cookout, talking about life and business…she was plotting their deaths.

"Girl...I," Healy was at a loss for words as well. "That man turned your husband into a monster!"

"Monster is a relative term, Doc," Ashley said. "My husband's a survivor. Unlike the rest of you."

The hybrid filtered water through its gills. Light had entered the dark tunnel where it swam. With the light came vibration. Voices! The steel barriers that prevented it from escaping during its entrapment had now been opened. It took in the familiar smells of its artificial environment.

It ascended, stopping just a few feet under the surface. It saw the four men, speaking to the bright light on the wall. It saw the face of the one who had spoken to it all these years, and recognized his voice. His artificial presence had the attention of all four of its targets. It just needed to wait for the right moment to strike.

The one with the shotgun stood the closest. Its attention was on the screen. The others were a few steps away. The problem that presented was minimal. The beast remembered the injury from its last attack, and was now determined to even the score.

It slowly ascended to the surface, its eyes fixed on the nearest human. It poised its body like a praying mantis, ready to strike.

Zimmerman crossed his arms, watching the bizarre conversation taking place. How this woman could turn so psychopathic, he had no idea. At least now they wouldn't waste time looking for her. The urge to escape surged through his mind. He felt a type of 'sixth sense' that he learned from recon—a sense he was being watched.

He turned around. The room was empty. No movement. Still no sign of that damn tunnel that led to the dock. All he noticed was that the water seemed darker. No...not darker, something was *in it!* WATCHING him! He saw the eyes, the crest, teeth, and poised arms.

His attempt to raise his shotgun paled to the speed of the creature's attack.

Rick, Healy, and Atkins turned to the sound of splashing water. As though vaulted from a catapult, the creature sprang at Zimmerman. His shotgun spiraled in midair like a baton after being knocked from his grasp. Pointed claws pierced his flesh and hooked into a firm grip. The merc let out a scream, which was quickly drowned out as the beast pulled him back into the pool.

The other three rushed to the pool's edge, and already, it was clouding red with Zimmerman's blood.

The creature wrestled him to the bottom, pinning him onto his back. Using its bodyweight to trap its prey, it plunged all ten fingertips into the mercenary's belly. Blood bubbles spewed from Zimmerman's mouth as the claws pulled outward, peeling his stomach open. Clouds of blood ascended from the open wound like smoke from a fire. The beast closed its head on the human's face, shredding the nose and cheek with its teeth.

Rick couldn't see through the blood cloud, but it was more than obvious that the mercenary was beyond help. The water swirled as the beast they knew as Danny proceeded to slaughter the merc.

He looked back to a mechanical sound, and realized that the door was closing. The doctor was locking him in!

"Son of a—" he scooped up Zimmerman's shotgun and sprinted as fast as he could. The two sides were just a couple of feet apart. He jammed the shotgun in-between them, lodging the barrel and the stock against the edges. The doors groaned, the gears struggling to push further. Already, the weapon began to fold. They only had seconds before it gave way to the pressure.

"Come on! Let's go before we're trapped in here!"

"You go first, Doc," Atkins said, pushing Healy forward. The medic ducked under the shotgun and proceeded into the corridor. By the time Atkins ducked under, the weapon was starting to crumple into a V-shape.

Rick glanced back one last time at the screen, his expression displaying a contempt for Ashley Rhee he never thought he'd feel. She smiled, seeing her husband beginning to emerge from the pool. Rick sprinted through the door, then kicked the shotgun out to let the doors latch shut. They closed another few inches but stopped on their own, likely from Dr. Berente's interference.

"Go!" he shouted to the others. As they retreated down the passageway, Rick glanced back to the doors. On the other side of the eighteen-inches of space was Danny, smiling with serrated teeth. He pressed his claws to the sliding doors and pushed them aside, then entered the passageway.

Dr. Wallace Berente smiled, watching the three survivors fleeing back toward the labs. Sharing his pride was Ashely Rhee. There was a glee in her eyes as she watched her husband, alive and fully functional, getting his revenge on the ones who betrayed him.

Let them run. Let them think they can escape.

Berente reached for the control panel with his fully functional hand. With a press of a button, he stripped the elevator unit of its power. There was no escape for them now. All he and Ashley had to do was sit and watch.

"You can run, but there's nowhere to hide."

CHAPTER 24

Thunderous rifle blasts echoed through the corridor. Rick Eilerman gritted his teeth, firing multiple three-round bursts at the creature. His ears felt like hammers pounding into his head from the condensed soundwaves.

His shots struck Danny in the chest. The beast screeched angrily from each blow. They weren't enough to break his exoskeleton, but the stopping power slowed his pursuit.

They were less than a hundred yards from the med-lab.

"The door's open. Move! Come on!" Atkins said. Rick fired another burst, hitting the hybrid in the throat. It lurched as though in pain, then roared like a prehistoric beast. It was angry now, and picking up speed. Rick aimed for its open mouth and squeezed the trigger.

"Shit, I'm out."

Healy grabbed him by the collar and shoved him ahead, then blasted his submachine gun. Bullets chipped its shell, but it didn't slow. All they could do was outrun it. He turned and sprinted with the others.

The medic could feel the thing gaining on him. He could feel the floor shuddering under its weight. The med-lab was directly ahead. Atkins dashed through it and immediately stood by the controls. Rick was through next.

Healy pushed himself as far as he could, but his knees felt like they were in a decompression chamber. He felt a heavy pop, and despite his will to survive, he went tumbling face-first to the floor. Cursing various phrases, he crawled for the entrance.

The beast closed the distance and reared his claws like spears, ready to impale its victim.

Both Atkins and Rick, their weapons loaded with fresh magazines, switched to full-auto, unleashing a deadly volley of bullets into Danny's torso. The hybrid screamed, the force chipping away at his protective shell. Bits of fragments hit the floor around its feet. It staggered backward, giving Healy just enough time to crawl for the door.

His magazine spent, Rick reached and grabbed the medic by his vest and pulled him through. Danny sprinted, claws outstretched, a violent scream blasting from his lungs. Atkins hit the access-control, slamming the door shut. It slid into place and latched, then dented outward as Danny crashed into it. He roared angrily, then bashed the door again.

Atkins fired a shot into the access control, permanently locking the door.

"That'll only hold him for so long," Healy said.

Atkins agreed. "No shit. Never thought I'd say this, but let's get back up to that forest."

They helped Healy up and helped him through the labs all the way to the elevator. Rick hit his fist on the button and waited. No response from the machine. He hit it again. Still nothing.

They heard the creature bashing the door. Folding metal creaked, gradually succumbing to the abuse. Rick tapped the button repeatedly.

"Come on, you son of a bitch!" He looked around, then noticed some of the mechanisms were no longer powered on. The filtration systems were switched off for the aquariums, and the strange storage container was no longer lit. "Goddamnit; Berente killed the power to this section."

"Great. We're fucking TRAPPED!" Atkins blared. He kicked the elevator doors, then paced back toward the med-lab, seeing the sealed metal doors to the left. No harm in checking again. He searched for an access control panel. Anything at all that looked like it would get that door open. But he found nothing. He tried to wedge his fingers through the slit where the two mechanical doors met, but it was no use. *Fucking door is just like my ex-wife.*

Another smash echoed through the labs. Atkins peeked through the juncture and saw the doors beginning to bend outward. He heard Danny sniffing like a dog. A moment later, his big black eye peered through the gap he had created. Atkins raised a middle finger at him.

"Remember *this*, buddy?"

The beast responded by body slamming the doors, weakening them further. Atkins retreated back to the aquarium lab.

"Yeah, we've got a minute or two at best. We're not getting this door open."

"Think we can blast it open?" Rick asked. Atkins examined the doors. They were thick, though not blast resistant.

"Hard to say. If we had a rocket launcher, I'd say yes. But all we have are grenades."

Rick removed his one remaining grenade from his vest. "Might as well give it a try."

Healy and Atkins took theirs out and placed them by the door. The mercenary briefly had a thought about tossing them into the corridor with the creature. A second glimpse at the widening door made him think otherwise. He'd have to have a pitcher's aim to get the grenades through there, otherwise, he'd have to get up close…within arm's reach. Exactly what their old friend Danny would love.

The three men placed their grenades at the base of the door, pulled the pins, then dashed for the med-lab, while cupping their hands over their ears. Five seconds later, the grenades exploded in unison. Aquarium glass shattered. Alarms rang out overhead and deep in other places within the facility.

The shockwave threw Danny in an uproar. He pounded his hands against the door edges, peeling them outward like onion slices. The gap was wide enough for him to stick his head through now.

His former teammates raced back to examine their escape route. Healy limped on both legs, appearing like a man twice his age as he followed the others.

"Damn it!" Atkins shouted, seeing the doors only slightly bent inward. He shoved his body against them and pushed with all his might. The doors shook, but refused to bend to his will. There was a small gap made between them, but it was insufficient for passage. Atkins gave up and angrily kicked the door. "Alright, we're fucked. Let's form a firing line. Maybe we'll hit it enough to break through its shell before it gets all of us."

"Wait, Angelo," Rick said.

"There's nothing to wait for except that thing," Atkins said. "We can't get through that door without explosives. All we had were our grenades, and they weren't enough."

"There's something else we can try," Healy said.

"What? Prybar?" Atkins remarked. The creature roared again. The door crumpled. They had seconds before it was through. Despite his arthritis-ridden knees, Healy rushed past the merc into the OR rooms.

"Help me with this!"

The two men followed him, surprised to see him handing them cannisters of anesthetic.

"What? We gonna gas the thing?" Rick said.

"That's a thought," Healy said. "Won't be able to do that without gassing ourselves, unfortunately. Get these by the door. And grab that oxygen tank!"

"What's the idea?" Atkins asked.

"This is cyclopropane. Pressurized. With a little bit of oxygen mixed in, and given a touch of flame, this stuff will put you to sleep in a way it wasn't necessarily intended." Neither man offered him any argument. They placed the cannisters near the partially busted door. "Get back."

Rick and Atkins rushed into the med-lab. The creature was almost through the door now. It peeked its face through again, baring teeth at its victims. They fired their rifles at it, driving it back.

Atkins fired another couple of rounds through the gap. Danny roared in defiance, and smashed the edges again, molding them into steel mounds.

"Hate to rush you, Healy, but..."

"Shut up..." Healy replied. Using tubing, he transferred oxygen into each of the tanks. He needed a flame. There were plenty of chemicals in the lab. Unfortunately, to get the reaction he needed, it would take time he didn't have. He would just have to use his gun and hope the bullet would produce a spark when breaching the cannister.

He hurried back into the med-lab and saw the beast about to step through the corridor entrance.

"Okay, somebody blast one of the cannisters...and take cover!" He ducked behind the table with the arm and covered his ears. Rick fired one last burst at the beast, then ducked behind the medic, while Atkins lined up a shot.

Oh, boy, this is gonna be loud, isn't it?

He fired a shot. The bullet hit one of the cannisters, sparking a brief flame, which ignited the cyclopropane. Suddenly, Atkins was on his back, tossed into the OR hall, his ears ringing and his vision blurred. The blast shook the building, bursting pipes, shredding ceiling panel, and absolutely devastating the chemical storage units.

Even with his hands cupped over their ears, Healy and Rick felt as though the world was spinning. Only from their training did they recognize the odors of several different gasses mixing in the room.

"Hope that blast got the door open, because we'll be dead in thirty seconds one way or another," Healy groaned. He hobbled to the door, and was relieved to see that both metal doors had been completely ravaged by the cannisters.

Rick grabbed Atkins by the vest and lifted him off the floor.

"Hold your breath," he warned.

"Put me down, I can walk," the merc spat. They joined the medic at the exit and gazed down the long corridor to Operations. They could hear alarms ringing all throughout the facility. They could see electrical panels spitting red sparks. The blast had rocked the entire compound.

The men leapt over the debris, escaping the deadly cloud of gas.

With one final blow, Danny smashed a hole through the doors and sprinted into the med-lab, only to immediately take in the deadly chemical cloud. He roared, his lungs and gills burning. He took another step, thinking he could rush through it and follow his victims. But the cloud stung his eyes and burned his shell to the touch. His nerves lit up like sirens, sending emergency signals to his brain.

Going through this cloud would only result in certain death. The beast turned back and raced for the pool, needing to cleanse his body of the filthy chemicals and embrace the warm air outside.

Rick kept his rifle pointed forward as he ran through the passageway. Though he glanced back to check whether Danny was following him, he had a new concern now.

This had been a trap. Berente *hoped* they'd come in; that way he and Ashley could gloat. But it was obvious he did not anticipate them escaping through this passageway—which now meant that Danny was no longer the only threat.

CHAPTER 25

"Goddamnit, Berente! I warned you about this!" Kruse shouted. Dr. Berente stared at the video feed, puzzled by the marines' successful escape from the lab. They were running straight for Operations now. Right for HIM. "Where the hell is the hybrid? Why isn't it pursuing?!"

"He has a name," Ashley snarled.

Kruse pointed a finger at her. "Not the time, lady." He turned and leaned down by Berente. Emergency lights spiraled overhead, creating a hellish glint on the doctor's glasses as he watched the few functioning screens. Several of them went black after the explosion. Those that functioned had a fuzzy picture quality. The camera near Staff Quarters and the conference rooms flickered, giving him footage just clear enough so he could see the prisoners. Danny was nowhere to be seen. The cameras in the labs were out, so he couldn't monitor his presence there. All he knew was that he was not pursuing.

"Is he alright?" Ashley said.

"I believe so," Berente said. "The blast probably created a cloud of chemical smoke. He probably retreated to his lair."

Kruse pushed the doctor aside and took his place at the controls. He attempted to initiate lockdown, but the doors were not responding.

"Goddamn it. There's no keeping them out," he said. He got on his radio. "Alright, gentlemen. Time to go to Plan B." Several mercenaries, armed with MP5 submachine guns, rushed into the room and took firing positions down the west door.

"What are you doing?" Berente said.

"Your game is over, Doctor," Kruse said. "It's time I do my job and eliminate these assholes."

"Danny can do that," Ashley said with a snarl. "That's why we're here. That's why we brought *them* here!"

"For the love of God, lady, we don't even know where he is," Kruse barked. "We can't lockdown this place. The blast shorted out our security systems. And I don't think those guys intend to have a simple chit-chat when they get in here. We need to get you out through one of the back tunnels." He turned and pointed to one of his men. "Take the scientist and the girl to Juncture Six and wait. Don't leave for the main dock until you hear from me."

"You want us to wait in the underground dock?" Ashley asked.

"Hey, if you want, you can take the elevator up and walk to the cliffs and climb the hatch. It's up to you. But it'll be faster if you take one of the Zodiacs."

"Oh, lovely," Ashley remarked. She hated the caves. It gave her a sense of being trapped. Especially at Juncture Six, where their underground dock connected the facility to the channel. Being too narrow for larger boats, only a few Zodiacs were stationed there. The original builders of this facility didn't bother to widen the cave. According to what she had heard, there had been a ceiling collapse during the construction of the elevator, which killed a few workers.

Kruse continued barking orders to his men. "I want four men with them. The rest of us will make quick work of these bastards. If anything goes wrong, get to the surface through Hatch Two or Four."

Ashley hit her fist against the console. "I waited *years* to see my husband get back at those assholes."

"Too bad," Kruse said. "Now get out of here, or be caught in the crossfire."

Dr. Berente stood up from his chair and guided Ashley to the back exit, escorted by four of Kruse's mercenaries. Kruse waited behind with eight of his men and took defensive position. Two of them stepped out and waited at the forward juncture, ready to ambush the targets as they came around the corner.

"They're getting close," he said. "Don't waste time on capturing them. As soon as you see movement, take them out."

Rick turned the corner into *Staff Quarters*. He passed several rooms full of bunks, all of which were empty. There was hardly even a hint that anyone had ever lived here, aside from the doctor himself.

The blast had severely damaged the compound. Wires flickered overhead, doors were stuck open, and emergency lights danced. He led the group down the next passageway. Directories on the ceiling pointed the way to Operations.

They were almost there, just another fifty feet and a left turn at the juncture.

Rick stopped and hugged the wall. The spiraling light around the corner up ahead betrayed the shadow of a crouched figure waiting just out of sight. He watched the flickering image, which was barely recognizable in the maddening strobes.

Rick looked up at the ceiling. There were four emergency lights in this section of the corridor. He pointed his rifle high and blasted each one, coating the group in darkness.

The mercenary jumped at the sound of the gunshots, then realized the corridor had gone dark. He looked to his partner, who was positioned in the corridor next to him. Simultaneously, they realized the prisoners were using the dark as cover—they KNEW they were waiting.

The two mercenaries leapt around the corner, ready to spray bullets into the corridor.

But Rick and Atkins had already closed the distance. They emerged from the dark and plunged their knives into the mercenaries' throats, then pulled them back into the darkness.

It was like witnessing a flash of lightning. In one instant, the marines were there, and suddenly, they disappeared around the corner, taking his men in tow.

All weapons were fixed on the doorway. Nobody would be able to do so much as peek without taking a round in the face.

"Well done," Kruse shouted. "Shooting out the lights. Very original. Won't help you when you come around that corner." Rick offered no response. "Oh? Nothing to say? Why don't you just step out and stop wasting my time?"

Behind the corner, Rick couldn't help but chuckle, as he and Atkins stripped the grenades off the dead mercenaries. They carried three each—more than enough to ruin a man's day—especially if he was in an enclosed area.

"Batter up," Atkins remarked. He and Rick unpinned four of the grenades and tossed then around the corner.

The mercenaries scattered, seeing the grey metal objects bouncing off the ceiling and scattering over the room. Kruse looked down as one landed by his foot.

"Fucking shit—" he dove behind the instrument panel. Four deafening cracks shook the room, shattering all lights except one. Dead mercenaries hit the floor, their bodies riddled with shrapnel, their organs displaced by the concussion.

Kruse stood up, barely managing to balance himself. Five of his men were dead, the remaining six in disarray. Another loud crack rang out, and another mercenary fell, blood spurting from the exit wound in his back. Rick, Atkins, and Healy stormed Operations, blasting away at the stunned mercenaries. Some fired back, barely able to see the marines in the dark room.

Grunting and cursing with each breath, Atkins retreated for the back door. Rick blasted another mercenary through the eyes, then saw the leader making his escape. He turned and fired, his bullet missing by a millimeter.

Damn!

As he started to pursue, another mercenary stepped out of the corridor and aimed his MP5 into the room. Rick hit him with three rounds to the chest, driving him backward. A few rounds fired into the ceiling as the merc spun and died.

As Healy neutralized a hostile near the large monitor panel, Atkins charged the last man standing, who had retreated to the back left corner of the room. The merc stood up on a computer desk and spun around to fire at the advancing marine, who already had his M4 pointed. Atkins fired a shot through the man's skull, the exit wound splattering the wall with pink.

Rick peeked into the back entrance, ready to unload into Kruse. He could hear the mercenary's footsteps retreating far down the corridor. He could hear other footsteps as well, some advancing, others moving away with their leader. There was another way out somewhere down this passageway, and they would certainly meet resistance along the way.

"This way," he said. Atkins and Healy followed him into the passageway and made a right turn into a brightly lit corridor. An emergency generator had kicked on, powering this side of the compound.

Running straight toward them were two mercenaries. Behind them were four others, and behind them was Kruse.

"Kill those pricks!" the mercenary leader shouted, then disappeared into the next juncture.

Rick fired several rounds at the two nearest targets. They danced in place, absorbing the bullets, before falling to the ground. Atkins stepped around the Sergeant and tossed one of the remaining grenades far into the hall. His throw was perfect, setting the explosive right in the center of the group. Two of the men managed to sprint out of the blast radius, while the other two did not react fast enough. The grenade detonated, launching both of them backward.

The two survivors stumbled, then fired a few rounds into the juncture. Rick ducked back. The bullets intended for him struck the corner, splintering it. Atkins dove to the left and aimed for the man on the left. He fired from the hip, his rounds sawing the mercenary across the waist. Healy emerged from the corner and fired a burst into the other. Bullets hit the target's upper torso, splintering breastbone and ravaging the heart and lungs.

"Good shot, Doc. Proceed down this corridor," Rick said. He took the lead again, stepping over bodies as he made his way to the next juncture.

Another merc waited around the corner. Rick started to turn, saw him, and reacted by diving back. Several shots zipped past him and struck the wall to his right. Rick turned the corner again and returned fire. The mercenary jolted as though hit with electricity, then fell into a pool of his own blood.

Kruse was a few hundred feet down the corridor, his running footsteps generating a series of distorted echoes. He turned on his heel and fired a few shots at the marines.

They hit the floor and fired back. With bullets striking the bulkheads around him, Kruse retreated into the next juncture.

"Kill those motherfuckers!" he shouted. As the three marines closed the distance, four more mercenaries appeared from the corner.

Rick found an alcove in the wall for an electrical breaker and dove inside. His two teammates hugged the opposite wall, pressing themselves behind piping. Several shots struck near them, one grazing Atkin's left leg.

Rick peeked around the edge and fired. A pink cloud burst from one of the mercenary's skulls. As he collapsed to the floor, Rick focused his fire on the other three, forcing them to go for cover. With no cover between here and the juncture, Atkins and Healy stormed the juncture.

One of the mercs tried to pull off a shot, which proved to be a fatal flaw. As Rick Eilerman had trained his team in years past, know INSTANTLY when to act. As soon as he saw the merc's brow, he unleashed a series of bullets, carving the man's face open. He could hear the others backing away.

Atkins and Healy each took a side, then stormed through the entrance, their guns blazing wildly. Bullets tore up the small hexagonal chamber, and the two standing mercenaries inside. Blood popped from their chests and backs, leaving behind shredded heaps that were once guns-for-hire.

It was a small space, only seven feet in diameter. To their surprise, it wasn't a corridor intersection, but a hatch chamber. On the righthand side was a ladder that led all the way to the surface.

"A way out?" Healy asked.

"Let me check," Rick said. He slung his rifle over his shoulder and ascended the thirty feet length of the ladder, reaching the hatch. He turned the wheel and pushed, but it wouldn't go. The welding patches along the sides caught his attention.

"Damn it, it's welded shut," he replied. No doubt, a concerted effort by Kruse to keep them confined in the corridor. Another shot rang out. Atkins heard the whistle of a bullet zipping in from the opposite entrance where they arrived. He peeked into the continuing corridor, then immediately ducked back as the group of mercenaries converged. There were eight of them, four in the corridor, four in the next juncture seventy-feet down.

"Can you shoot it open?" Atkins said. He reloaded his weapon and fired into the hall, striking one of the mercs. He ducked back as the others returned fire. Rick examined the latches.

"A well-placed grenade would probably do it. Problem is, there's nowhere for me to secure it," he said.

Atkins grunted. *And we can't get out without putting ourselves in the line of fire.*

"Looks like we'll have to party with these assholes a little longer." He aimed his rifle around the corner and fired another burst.

CHAPTER 26

The beast was no stranger to darkness. Many times during his development, he had been deliberately kept in blackness. The conditioning enhanced his other senses, allowing him to exploit his new abilities, and effectively kill the human mind beneath. Not so much memory or intelligence, but compassion and empathy—the humanity that separated him from the genes of creatures that had blended with his own.

Danny swam through the tunnel, allowing the water to seep through his gills. His superior strength allowed him to sprint through the jungle despite his three-hundred pounds. Swimming, however, still took a little bit of conditioning. He could feel the current of the main tunnel up ahead. Using his claws, he clung to the tunnel wall and climbed the rest of the way like an insect.

It entered the junction where the tunnel connected with the cave. He saw lights further in. And voices! There were at least a dozen people down there. Danny swam, keeping a few feet below the surface. Up ahead was a large dock with two boats secured near it. He swam under the boats, silent as a ghost, then very slowly emerged near one of the support beams, under the ledge. He peered up through the cracks, stalking the humans, deciding which he'd kill first. Humans moved overhead, the ones in black armed with automatic weapons. Danny's instinct to kill was like a hunger that could never be satisfied.

He stopped, recognizing one of the voices. It was his master; his savior. He spoke to somebody, who replied back. There was a female in the group. Curiosity overcame the intense desire to kill. There was something about that voice that was familiar as well. Distant memories fogged Danny's mind. It wasn't just *any* female voice. Something was special about this one.

Danny kept his movements slight to keep from stirring the water and betraying his presence. He moved further down the dock and gazed up again. He saw golden skin and sparkling amber hair. Suddenly, his urge to kill had vanished completely. It was *her!* His wife. A tsunami of memories soared through his brain. He hadn't seen Ashley in years…not since his last deployment.

He remembered home. He remembered Oregon. Their truck. Their backyard. Their house. He could feel the sensation of their bed on his soft skin…when it wasn't crustacean. He remembered their lips touching, the pleasure he felt when they were naked together in the heat of romance. All the things that were taken away because his 'friends' left him to die.

But even the thought of them didn't fuel his desire to kill. He watched her through the boards, experiencing a strange state of peace. She stood near the edge of the dock, staring out into the tunnel as the others spoke. It was as if her very presence was angelic to him, calming the monster within. In this moment, he wasn't a wild creature with a taste for blood. He was Danny Rhee, gazing at his beautiful wife, whom he didn't realize how much he missed.

Sadly, her angelic demeanor didn't last. Behind her, a steel door opened, and a towering figure stepped out onto the dock.

Ashley crossed her arms, staring into the far reaches of the cave. She felt like she was in the throat of some enormous monster. The lights around the dock only stretched so far before the distance became nothing but black. As the mercenaries prepped the boats, she couldn't help but glance at the elevator on her right. She had to remind herself of all the wildlife up above, which included venomous species of snakes and arachnids.

She heard the door open behind her. Kruse stepped out, breathing heavily, in the process of reloading his rifle.

"What's happening?" Berente asked.

"We're gonna have to get you to the yachts," Kruse said.

"You can't handle *three* men?" Berente said. He laughed, condescendingly. "You and all these soldiers you have working for you? And I was told you were the best!"

"And I was told your fishman out there would have these guys within an hour of their arrival," Kruse retorted. "TWICE it failed. And you, doctor, allowed these men to come into this facility and fuck up our operation. Now they're running around, with weapons you and your clients provided, killing my men! All for what? To stroke your ego? To show off your precious pet to these idiots?"

"I'm sick of your remarks," Ashley snapped. "It's a *him*. He's not a pet. He's my husband!"

"Oh, right. You're *SO* in love!" Kruse spat. "That totally explains why you fucked his best friend—how many times?"

"Shut up," Ashley said, her voice low and threatening. "I did that to set him up for you. That was the plan. You all know it."

"Right. Only needed to do it that one night. But haven't you been fucking him for like a month leading up to that? I think somebody really enjoyed having Mr. Rick Eilerman's big dick throbbing between her legs."

Ashley slapped him across the face. One of the mercenaries stepped forward to restrain her, but caught an unexpected elbow to the chin, knocking him back. His heel scratched the edge of the dock. One of his companions grabbed him by the vest, stopping him from tumbling into the water.

"Fuck, lady!"

A loud roar thundered beneath their feet.

Several realities plunged into Danny's mind like knives. His beloved wife had betrayed him. Not only had she been unfaithful, but she had been unfaithful with Rick Eilerman! His former best friend. The man who left him to die! And these men had set her up to do it! The mercenary! The doctor!

The brief spark of humanity that shined when he saw Ashley had erupted into a blazing fire, determined to destroy anything around it.

In a blaze of anger, Danny plowed his fists up through the dock. A spectacle of broken deck boards erupted, creating a gaping hole in the dock. Danny hauled himself up through the breach like an insect springing onto a fresh leaf.

"Jesus!" a terrified mercenary screamed. His defensive reflex was automatic. Bullets tore from the muzzle of his submachine gun and struck the hybrid's shell. Danny, enraged further, turned to his right and lashed at the mercenary. Fingers slashed his throat, spinning the mercenary to his left, gun still discharging. One of his companions took several rounds in the stomach, while the others scattered. The mercenary, still barely conscious, continued to spin on his heel, unwittingly discharging his gun at the Zodiacs. Bullets punctured the fuel tanks, sparking and igniting the fuel.

The explosion uprooted the whole edge of the dock, sending the mercenary flying backward…right in to Danny's arm. The hybrid snarled; he wasn't done with this merc. Straightening his fingers into spear-tips, he plowed his claw through his back. Bone-hard fingertips prodded out of the merc's belly before retracting out his back. Spraying blood from his throat and midsection, the merc plopped into the water.

More gunshots rang out, striking Danny's back and shoulder. He whipped around, bellowed, then charged his next victim. The mercenary backed away and screamed, his bullets doing little more than chipping at the monster's chest. Danny smashed both claws around his head then twisted repeatedly. The mercenary's body twitched, his neck snapping, then detaching completely. Danny turned to his right, holding the severed head of his victim at Kruse and his two remaining mercenaries.

Kruse focused his aim at the hybrid's left shoulder joint and fired. Danny's roar was high-pitched, blood splattering from the vulnerable fibrous tissue. He tossed the head and lashed out. Kruse backstepped, unwittingly passing one of his men, who stood frozen in fear. Danny redirected his focus on the nearer target and lunged. Claws slashed deep into his belly. The merc didn't even register the pain as much as he did the sudden drop in weight, as his intestines and stomach spilled out onto the deck. Shocked at the sight of his own insides, the merc dropped to his knees, eyes fixed on the horrifying, yet oddly spectacular sight.

Danny watched the dying man for a moment, then directed his gaze straight ahead. Ashley had backed all the way to the far side of the dock, hands covering her mouth in fear.

"Danny?" she whispered. He watched her for a moment, cocking his head like a bird. He couldn't help but stare at his wife. His beloved. His *betrayer.*

Seeing the creature distracted, Kruse dashed for the tunnel entrance. It saw him move in its peripheral vision and turned, seeing Kruse already on one knee, weapon aimed high. A single shot struck his crest, knocking his head back. A horrifying roar of titanic proportions shook the room.

Kruse unloaded into the beast, only agitating it further. Realizing his mistake, he retreated back into the tunnel.

"Fucking shit!" he said to himself. He could hear Danny's heavy feet strike down on the metal flooring behind him. The beast was charging, jaws dripping saliva, ready to peel the flesh from his bones.

Ashley gasped as her husband chased the mercenary into the facility.

"Danny?" she said. Berente grabbed her by the shoulder, stopping her.

"Let him go," he said. "As you can see, they're no match for him. Come with me. We'll go to the boats just to be safe."

Ashley looked at the blazing fire around the dock.

"How do we get there?"

"We'll take the elevator to the surface and head to the cliffs by foot," Berente explained. "There's a hatch behind the tree line near the cave. There's a ladder there. We'll climb down and board a yacht. I'll continue to monitor the situation with drones and wireless camera feeds. We'll know when Danny's done killing everybody."

Ashley caught her breath, then nodded. "Okay."

She followed the doctor into the elevator, which lifted them up through the roof of the cave all the way to the surface. When the doors opened again, she was looking out into the jungle. Sunlight beamed into the compartment, almost blinding her.

"This way," Berente said. They went out into the jungle and made their way southwest.

****

Bullets flew without mercy, battering the small juncture where the marines were held up. Healy hugged the hatch door, flinching as bullets bounced off the walls. Atkins stuck his rifle barrel through the corner and fired aimlessly. Unfortunately, he couldn't do so much as peek around the corner without getting hit.

"Maybe they'll run out of bullets one of these days," he remarked.

"One can only hope," Rick said. Clinging tight to the ladder bar, he banged the butt of his rifle against the welding patches, hoping they were weak enough to come apart. "No good. I could try shooting it."

"Not unless you want those bullets to ricochet and bite you in the gut," Atkins said. He fired another burst. Enemy fire struck his muzzle, jamming the barrel. "Shit!" He lifted his finger from the trigger, barely avoiding blowing the weapon up in his face. It was useless now.

Healy took his place and fired a few shots into the corridor. Atkins tossed his dead rifle aside and grabbed an MP5 from one of the dead mercs.

They both heard something bouncing and rolling along the floor toward them. One thing was certain: it was no tennis ball.

The grenade passed through the entrance and settled two feet from Healy's boots.

"FUCK!"

The medic kicked it back into the corridor, then dove back behind the corner. The grenade burst, causing some dismay among the mercenaries. Healy took the opportunity to aim properly, placing several rounds right below the target's neckline. He squeezed off another few shots, forcing the other mercenaries in the corridor to withdraw into the juncture. Atkins took the other side of the entrance and unleashed a few rounds. Another mercenary hit his knees and skidded into the juncture, while bleeding from several holes in his back. He got off another shot before another volley of bullets forced him and Healy behind cover.

"It's a bottleneck. Unfortunately, they've got more guns than us," Healy said. He looked up at Rick. "Any luck on that hatch?"

"They've got it sealed tight," Rick replied.

"Or you suck," Atkins replied, reloading his MP5. He was grinning—he'd rather shoot his way out anyway. More fun. For once, Rick appreciated that attitude, as there was no other option.

With his Desert Eagle propped between his palms, Kruse ran down the hallway, only a few paces ahead of the rampaging beast. He fired the pistol over his shoulder in vain hope that it would slow the beast down. He followed the passageway toward the sound of gunfire.

Danny snarled, his clawed toes scratching the metal flooring with each step. The prey was almost within reach. Its futile attempt to flee would've made him laugh, had Danny retained his sense of humor after the transition. But now, it was gone, as were many of his human characteristics. His last connection to humanity had betrayed him in the worst way. All that he was, what he had, only to be replaced by an unquenchable desire to kill. It was an itch that could never be scratched. Each death was never enough—it just only required more. Like the worst of drugs.

The passageway curved to the right. Kruse kept up the pace. He had to make it to the next juncture. It was a three-way intersection with a path that would lead straight to Hatch four.

The gunfire grew louder as he approached. The passageway straightened into a straight shot to the next juncture. He could see his men bunched in there, shooting down the hall where the prisoners were holed up.

"Disperse! Out of the way!" he shouted. Several pairs of eyes turned toward him, then widened at the sight of the monstrosity racing right behind him. Kruse had no choice. If he slowed even the tiniest bit, he'd be snatched up. There was no choice; he ran straight into the juncture.

Danny followed him to the edge of the juncture, slowing only to decide which of the humans to kill. Kruse turned to the left and ran into the next passageway.

"Come on!" he yelled to the mercs. But the bloodbath had already begun. Danny speared one of the mercenaries with his claws and lifted him up to his mouth. He hyperextended his shark-like jaws and sank his teeth into the skull. The pair of jaws closed like a vice, slicing off the mercenary's entire face from the forehead to the chin.

He tossed the body aside then raced at his next victim. A swing of his arm slit the mercenary's throat. Blood sprayed the juncture, bullets flying aimlessly from his MP5. The enclosed space descended into chaos, with mercenaries trying to evade both bullets and a ravaging beast.

One fired his weapon point-blank into Danny's abdomen, only to have the bullets bounce back and slice through his own. He gasped in pain, then dropped to his knees, splashing in the newly formed puddle of blood. Two of the mercenaries followed Kruse into the connecting passageway, while one last remaining merc sprayed rounds at the hybrid. Danny smacked the gun from his grasp, then lifted the merc against the wall. His arms and legs flailed, as though each was an individual entity trying to escape the terror. Danny opened his jaws and leaned in.

The mercenary screamed. "No! No! NOOOO!" The jaws closed over his midsection and ripped away a mouthful of guts. Danny swallowed and bit again. Intestines and stomach contents poured at his feet. The flailing arms fell slack. Danny tossed his victims aside, then followed the sound of running feet into the adjoining corridor.

"Shhh…" Atkins whispered, peeking around the corner. He had watched as Danny slayed the barricading force that had them pinned, then ran out of sight to pursue Kruse. It seemed that his allegiance to Berente's staff was gone, if there even was one to begin with. He was a rampaging monster on the loose, slaughtering anyone that found themselves in his path.

Rick slid down the ladder and followed his friends into the passageway. They approached the next juncture with caution, then stepped through to continue to the dock zone. They could hear a mixture of screams, roars, and gunfire down the connecting passageway.

"Well, we definitely don't want to go *that* way," Rick said.

"No fucking shit," Atkins remarked. They continued down the south corridor to make their way to Juncture Six.

Danny felt a hellish delight as he impaled the mercenary with his claws and slammed him against the wall. He savored the kill, slowly pulling his claws to the side. The mercenary yelled and stretched, as though somehow that would free him from the two hands in his belly.

Kruse stopped only long enough for a glance. In that split second, he witnessed the gunman's midsection split open, and everything trapped inside fall free in a soupy mess. The mercenary leader was only a hundred feet off Hatch Four. He could see the ladder straight ahead. He sprinted as fast as he could, outpacing the one other survivor.

With a bounding leap, he threw himself onto the ladder bars and ascended. With a few pulls he was already ten feet up, with twenty more to go. His minion was right below him. His hands had just touched the ladder bars when he heard the creature drop his comrade's body. Running feet grew loud and near. Against his better judgement, the mercenary looked back. All sense of training left him, and he simply threw his arms over his eyes and screamed for dear life.

Danny slashed his belly, then his face. He wrestled the mercenary to the floor, then hacked at the back of his neck as though his claw was a hatchet. Bone snapped and flesh peeled.

Kruse reached the hatch and pushed it open. He glanced down the ladder, just in time to see his subordinate's head roll free from his shoulders. The beast looked at him, jaws and hands stained with red. It snarled at him, then began climbing the ladder.

Kruse pulled himself into the jungle and sealed the hatch. There was no seal; no way to keep the creature from coming out. There was no choice other than to flee. There was only one way off this island, and that was the boats under the southwest cliffs.

He only completed five strides before the hybrid burst the hatch door off its frame. Blood dripped from Danny's fingers as he lifted himself onto the grass. Little meaty hairs dangled from his teeth as he gazed at the retreating human. There was no stopping now. He had accepted the fate of being a mindless killing machine. Anything…*everything* in his path, he would kill.

"Holy shit," Atkins heaved. When they arrived at the ravaged dock, it was as if they had breathed in chemical weapons. There was no oxygen in the cave; only smoke. All three men covered their mouths, fighting against the intense burning in their lungs while searching for a way out. The Zodiacs were destroyed, as was the entire side of the dock.

"How'd they get out?" Healy said. As soon as he stated the question, he noticed the elevator doors to his right.

Rick hurried over to them and activated the lift. They could hear the elevator descending from above.

"Hurry up," he coughed. Everything burned inside. Yet, they weren't going to wait in the tunnels, where Danny might be lurking. For all they knew, he could've heard their footsteps and doubled back. The elevator took its sweet time, as if it had a sick sense of humor.

"Come on, you piece of shit," Atkins said. It felt like a year had passed by when the doors finally opened up. All three men dashed inside. The doors closed tight, and the trio spent the entire ride up coughing and gagging. It was fifty-year old technology, and it showed. Still, it worked.

The doors opened, allowing fresh air and sunlight into the car. The three men rushed out. They never thought they'd be so happy to see the inside of this jungle again.

They coughed and spat, slowly relieving their burning insides. Had their senses not been compromised, they would've noticed the sound of running feet much sooner.

Kruse had heard the elevator compartment rise from the jungle floor. No way was that Berente and Ashley, as they had likely lifted out immediately after the thing attacked. No, it was the remnants of Fire Team Delta. The hybrid was a few meters behind him and closing. Despite his excellent stamina, Kruse was quickly being worn down. The only way to get rid of the beast would be to present something else for it to kill. And who better than the men who he had brought here for it to kill in the first place?

Two birds with one stone.

When he arrived, he saw smoke rising from the elevator. The three marines were coughing, having been trapped in a cave full of fumes. They were compromised. Unaware. Vulnerable.

Atkins was the first to look up. By the time he recognized the approaching mercenary, he heard the crack of the Desert Eagle, and simultaneously felt the round punch through his left shoulder. He spun on his feet and hit the ground. The running mercenary fired at the other two, who were sprinting out of the way. Bullets tore into the thick ferns around them.

Instead of pressing the attack, Kruse kept running, angling off to the right.

Atkins rolled to his side and sprayed bullets, but the merc had already disappeared into the jungle. Bleeding from his shoulder, he rolled to his knees, ready to chase the bastard down. Then he saw Danny.

The hybrid gazed at what remained of his old fireteam. His eyes focused on Rick Eilerman. Kruse's words to Ashley echoed in his memory. Rick wasn't just the one to leave him to die; on top of that, he fucked his wife!

All trace of Danny Rhee disappeared, dissolved into the fury of a carnivorous beast.

"Go!" Rick yelled to the others. He stood toe-to-toe with the approaching monster. "Danny! Danny! Stop!" He didn't. Danny raised his claws to slash his former Sergeant. In his fury, he didn't realize that while Rick was trying to talk him down, he was aiming his barrel at the chitin at his knees. Several shots rang out, and Danny suddenly dropped, roaring furiously. One of the bullets found its way into the soft fibrous tissue.

Atkins joined in on the assault, emptying the rest of his magazine into Danny's side. Most of the bullets smashed uselessly into his shell. One, however, managed to puncture one of the gill slits in Danny's neck, causing a thick stream of blood to burst out. Danny shrieked in agony, then leapt back to his feet. Atkins backtracked, surprised to see the hybrid still so agile despite its leg injury. He squeezed the trigger, but only heard *clicks*. With no fresh magazines, he flung the weapon at the creature's face. It did nothing other than momentarily jolt its head to the side.

It raised its hand to slash.

Bullets struck its knuckles, blasting two of its fingers clean off. Danny screamed and whipped around, only to take another barrage of bullets to the face. Rick and Healy stood side-by-side, firing in short controlled bursts. Both of them were on their last magazines.

A splash of blood exploded where Danny's right eye was. His head whipped to the side, whipping black fleshy strands. The wound continued to jet red, while other bullets crunched against his ribs and neck. Another one found its way through the gill slits. Blood spat from Danny's mouth.

Then, at once, both weapons ran dry.

"Shit," Healy said, dropping the now useless weapon. He and Rick ran past the creature, who was currently gasping for air.

Danny stumbled, half-blind. His regeneration attributes would heal his eye, but it didn't quell the fact that his vision was compromised. On top of that, he could barely breathe due to the bullets lodged in his neck. He was faced with a severe problem. His tissue would heal, but the fragments would still be there, partially blocking off his airway. He would need to operate on himself now to get the worst ones out, while he still had the entry wound to use as a guide. If he waited, the puncture would close, and he would have to guide his claw blindly, which would risk slicing several arteries. Even his accelerated healing wouldn't act in time to save him.

Danny fell on his hands and knees, propping himself on his injured right hand. He took his left index finger and inserted it through his gills. The pain hit instantly. The hybrid squealed as he reached further in. He found one of the fragments and pinched it with his finger and thumb.

The jungle swayed as the three men dashed through the vegetation. They weren't going to waste time with caution. There was no telling how many boats were on the docks, and they couldn't risk losing time in case Kruse and Berente took them.

"Southwest," Rick said, keeping track of the direction of the sunlight. The cliffs were much closer. Going to the Zodiac on the north end would take too long. He could smell the ocean. The sunlight was getting stronger. They were getting close. He looked back and noticed Healy was lagging behind. "You alright, man?"

"I've pushed my knees further than they were ever meant to go," Healy replied. The pain was obvious in his voice. It would take morphine at this point to dull the agony in his joints.

"It's alright. Once we're out we'll—" Rick turned forward and saw the mercenary, Kruse, peeking around a tree. There was an underhanded movement, as though he was tossing a softball…

…or a grenade.

It landed just a few feet to his left.

"Take cover!" All three men dove in opposite directions. The grenade exploded, shredding the vegetation surrounding it.

Atkins tried getting up. Warped vision and ringing ears seemed to be his new thing. He realized his hands were empty, his Beretta having bounced from his grip. He looked to where Kruse had appeared. He wasn't there anymore. Healy was facedown behind him, and Rick was a few feet straight ahead, stunned but still attempting to get up.

Atkins saw the shrubs ahead of his former Sergeant rustle. Stepping out from between them was Kruse, his Desert Eagle propped in his hands. He kicked Rick's Beretta from his grip, then aimed squarely at his forehead.

Not so fast!

Atkins unsheathed his knife and held it by the tip of the blade. There was no time for a good aim. He would just have to wing it. The knife zipped through the air and grazed Kruse's forearm. The laceration was nothing fatal, but it was enough to jolt the mercenary's aim to the right, the resulting gunshot discharging away from Rick's face. Atkins charged at the mercenary and kicked his foot as though putting a football. His toe struck the Desert Eagle under the muzzle, launching it from Kruse's grip.

The two men found themselves in a violent tussle, each man trying to outmuscle the other. Unfortunately for Atkins, however, he had an enemy who knew how to exploit injury. And he did so without hesitation. Kruse jabbed his thumb into Atkins' bullet wound, sparking screams of pain, as well as weakening his grip. Kruse followed up the attack with a kick to the knee, and an uppercut to the jaw. Atkins, refusing to go down, staggered backward. Dazed, and still somewhat stunned by the explosion, he swung wildly, only for Kruse to grab his arm and flip him over his shoulder.

A stomp to his groin caused Atkins to yell out, which was also stopped prematurely by a kick to the jaw. The blow rolled Atkins to his stomach. The world spun. He looked up, seeing three distorted images of Kruse standing above him. He unsheathed his knife, the blade glinting in the sunlight. He raised the knife high and brought it down. As the blade dropped within an inch, it and its owner were suddenly flung to the side.

Kruse fell on his back, then shook from the impact of Rick Eilerman's fist. The Sergeant landed several punches to the jaw, then grabbed the hand that wielded the knife. Kruse snarled, surprised and frustrated by his failure to outmuscle his enemy. He wrapped his other arm around Rick's shoulders and pulled, while simultaneously attempting to push the knife into his throat.

Still holding onto the merc's arm, Rick ducked and pivoted, locking Kruse's elbow behind his back. He kicked the back of his knee out, then shoved his face into the dirt. With a twist of his wrist, Rick pried the knife from Kruse's grip, then plunged the blade right into the small of his back.

Kruse screamed, feeling a pain that dwarfed anything he had ever endured in his life. Rick pushed the blade through his spinal column, then stood over his fallen enemy.

"You fuck! You son of a bitch! I'll rip your fucking heart out!" Kruse screamed. He floundered on the ground like a suffocating fish. Fingers curled as his nerves surged like electricity.

"Yeah, good luck with that," Rick replied. Behind him, Atkins was pulling Healy to his feet. On top of his other agonies, the medic had taken a few pieces of shrapnel to the ribs.

"I'm fine," he said, pulling himself away from Atkins. He approached the half-paralyzed mercenary. He flipped him over onto his back. Kruse tried to lash out, but his movements only resulted in more pain. Healy snatched a couple of grenades from his belt. "Thanks for these."

"Go ahead. Kill me," Kruse spat.

"Believe me, someone will," Atkins said. They looked back and heard approaching footsteps and raspy breathing. Danny was coming, and fast!

"Let's go!" Rick said. The trio of marines leapt over Kruse and continued retreating southwest.

The mercenary arched his back, squealing with each movement. The footsteps grew more intense. The jungle tore open, and the hybrid stood over him.

Blood drizzled from Danny's gills as he gazed at the wounded mercenary. Fallen. Paralyzed. Unarmed. Pathetic. Easy prey. He wasted no time attacking. Kruse thought he had experienced the worst pain of his life. He was wrong. He yelled, gargling blood, as jaws and fingers ripped away at his ribcage. Intestines uncoiled. Kidneys burst. Lungs deflated and came apart like cotton. A fountain of blood sprayed his own face. It was the last thing he'd ever taste.

Danny could hear the others. They weren't too far ahead. He would easily outrun them. They didn't have much ammo now. He wouldn't have to waste time with stealth. He wanted to get right to it: he wanted Rick Eilerman's head.

Healy couldn't go any further. He stumbled, lagging further and further behind. Even worse, he could hear Danny approaching from behind. He was closing in fast, and there was no way he'd outrun him. He looked at the grenades in his hands.

"Rick!" he shouted. Rick and Atkins turned around.

"Come on, Healy." Rick trembled as the medic tossed his Beretta and one of the grenades.

"Get going," Healy said. "I'll hold him off."

"Healy! Don't!" Rick said.

The medic had already turned around, using what remained of his endurance to race back toward the creature. Rick started to go after him, only for Atkins to grab him by the shoulders.

"He's gone, man. He's choosing this."

Rick took a deep breath and accepted the reality. It was a miracle that Healy even made it this far, despite his handicap. With the creature closing in, and almost no weapons to fight it with, the next encounter would be certain doom for all of them. Rick forced himself to accept this. Waiting here would only cheapen his sacrifice.

"Alight, let's go. We're not too far."

Danny leapt over the ruins of a fallen branch, then shredded the vegetation directly behind it. He emerged in a few feet of clearing, where one of his victims waited. It was Healy, the medic. He stood straight, breathing heavily, arms crossed as though he were impatiently waiting on Danny's arrival.

"I've had it with you, you prick. We were your friends. Your brothers. Now look at you. You're not Danny Rhee. You're something that ought to be served in *Red Lobster* with a set of walnut crackers."

Danny snarled, enraged. Clearly, Healy was buying time for the others. Good. Let him.

The hybrid sprang at the medic and pinned him to the ground. As he plunged his claws deep into his chest and ripped, he heard the familiar sound of safety levers releasing. Then he saw the grenades tucked under Healy's elbows.

Danny ripped his hands free then turned to run, only to be thrown by the twin detonations.

Rick and Atkins stopped momentarily after hearing the blast. It was only a moment's hesitation, allowing them to accept the fate of their companion.

It was almost over now. Kruse was dead. All there was left was Berente. And Rick was not going to let him get away with what he had done.

CHAPTER 27

Ocean waves broke into millions of individual droplets and molecules. Those molecules traveled high toward the cliff peak as a thick mist, which coated the face of the woman standing at its edge. Ashley watched the droplets fall back into the ocean, seamlessly becoming one body again.

The fluidity of water was part of Dr. Berente's pitch when he first got in contact with her regarding her husband's treatment. It seemed so alien at the time, having her husband's cells joined with those of the other species. But she had seen the photos. Danny was barely alive, his features almost gone from the intense burns. A normal life was not in the cards for him one way or another.

Ashley watched another set of swells break apart, only to rebuild, much like what had happened to her husband. He was alive due to this formula. Alive, and flourishing. She reminded herself of this right now, after hearing the horrible explosions and gunfire somewhere within the island. She had faith that her husband, her love, was successful in his revenge. If only she could've witnessed it.

Behind the trees behind her, Berente worked on opening the hatch. It hadn't been touched in years, which had caused the outside handle to rust shut. He banged on it with a log as best he could, despite his injured hand.

"May I ask you a question?" she asked.

"Now?" the doctor replied. His glasses were crooked, soaked in his sweat.

"Why haven't you fixed your arm?" she asked. "You've succeeded in regrowth and regeneration. Why haven't you regenerated your muscle tissue and fingers?"

Berente slammed the log on the hatch again, breaking off flakes of rust.

"Because I don't have anyone to treat me," he replied. "Self-treatment is not recommended in this case. I'd need a surgeon, someone to monitor me, keep my medications at the right level. There's a lot of pain and brain fog in the process, even with the anesthetic. If I treated myself, I'd more than likely make a mistake somewhere in the process because my senses would be compromised. Besides," he looked at his arm, "it reminds me of why I do this."

Ashley stepped closer, her stare an inquisitive one. Berente was feeling uncomfortable now, as if she suddenly regretted her husband's transformation.

"Or is it because of the mutation that comes with it?" she said. Berente wasn't sure whether to admit the truth or not.

"I saved your husband, damn it. I saved his *life*! After what he did to my lab! To my brother! I pulled him out of the fire with *this hand*. Had I not—"

"That's not what I'm getting at," Ashley said. Berente calmed.

"Then what?"

Ashley looked back at the jungle, hoping her husband would step out somewhere. Her gaze returned to the doctor.

"Could you change me?"

Berente was surprised. "Change *you?* You mean—to look like him?"

"Yes," she said. A smile came over her face. "It's for better or for worse, richer or poorer, till death do us part. If I'm gonna be with him, I want to be *like* him."

Berente hadn't considered this, but he could understand her reasoning.

"Mrs. Rhee, you're aware of the procedure, yes? It takes a while, and is extremely painful. Your whole genetic structure changes. Your skeletal structure mutates, which is more than most people can endure."

"I know that I couldn't endure losing him," she said. "I want our lives together again, even if that means changing everything about who I am."

Berente stood straight. "It will take a little time to repair the damage done to our facility. That said, if you so wish, I will make it happen."

"Good. Let it be soon," she said, breathing heavily. "I want this."

"Yeah, and people in Hell want milkshakes," Atkins shouted. Berente and Ashley jumped back from the hatch as the two men burst out of the jungle. Rick kept his pistol fixed on the doctor, who promptly raised his hands.

"I oughta put a bullet through that brain of yours, just like I did your little brother," he said.

"Why don't you? Clearly, you're not afraid of killing an unarmed man," Berente said.

The pistol twitched in Rick's hand. He wanted to. He REALLY wanted to. But he couldn't. The memory of killing Rex Berente haunted him ever since the mission, and not just because he lost Danny that day. It was the first time he'd ever executed an unarmed man, who was clearly willing to surrender, no less. It was different than killing an armed soldier in the midst of combat. And it was that action that led to all of this madness, regardless of the fact he was under orders, and that Rex was probably deserving of it. Hell, Wallace Berente was clearly MORE deserving of a shot to the skull. And leaving him alive would leave the door wide open for future mutations. Yet, Rick didn't want to revisit it.

"I guess I'm ready for that part of my life to be over," he said. He turned to Ashley, "But YOU! How could you have done this? What's gone into your brain?!"

"Danny's my husband. This was his only shot at survival!" Ashley said, her eyes welling up.

"That's not Danny," Atkins said. "Maybe it was at some point. But that's a bloodsucking carnivore. You think you two will have a life sitting at the kitchen table, discussing politics, and—" he left out the part with the bedroom.

"You'd probably prefer if he had died in that fire," Ashley said.

"Yes, actually, I would have. Compared to this," Rick replied. "If I could turn back time, believe me, I would've handled that infiltration differently. But hindsight is twenty-twenty, and I didn't have it then. And Danny died. The Danny I knew. I just didn't realize his wife died that same day."

"Where is he?" she asked. Her voice trembled. These two men shouldn't even be alive right now. She could hear the recent gunfire and explosions in her mind. Had Rick Eilerman killed her husband a second time? His lack of an answer worsened her anxiety. "WHERE IS HE?"

"Somewhere back there," Atkins said, cocking his head toward the forest behind him. Unlike Rick, he had no problem speaking bluntly to her.

"Is he alive?" Ashley was on the verge of hyperventilating.

Atkins shrugged. "Hard to say. Healy gave him a new birthday present. Same one I oughta give to you two. Oh, by the way, I appreciate you loosening the hatch for us. Saved us the trouble of doing it ourselves. Not to mention it made it easier to find it."

"Back away from it," Rick ordered. Berente wiped his lenses then placed them back over his face.

"You know, the offer on my recording still holds true," he said. "You've proven to be more capable than Kruse ever was. You've outwitted the hybrid. You have won. With my client's funds, I can make you richer than you've ever dreamed of. All you need to do is walk away."

"Walk away? I could've never come here…for *free*," Rick said.

"Just put a bullet in him, for godsake," Atkins said.

Rick aimed low and fired. A hole popped right under Berente's left kneecap. He shrieked and fell to the ground, hands clutching at his splintered shin.

"You bastard! You prick! You cockfucker!"

"Yeah, maybe I don't have it in me," Rick said. "But you know who *does?*" He handed the pistol over to Atkins, who did not hesitate to aim at Berente's head.

"NO!" Ashley screamed, throwing herself between the mercenary and the scientist. Gritting his teeth, Atkins jerked the weapon away, barely managing to keep from shooting her. Even despite what she had done to his friends, even *he* had difficulty fathoming the thought of shooting down Danny's wife.

"Get out of the way," he said. He stepped to the side, but she stepped with him, keeping Berente shielded.

Ashley smiled. "You won't do it."

"I will if you don't move," he said.

"Ricky there won't let you. Would you Rick? Not after all we've shared?" She brushed her hand around her neck seductively, working her hand down to her chest, her fingers gently tugging down the edge of her tank top.

"Yeah, not gonna work this time," Rick said. "I do remember you liking it rough." He grabbed her by the shoulders and yanked her out of the way. Her seductive demeanor changed into a screaming fit as she fought against him. Rick moved her aside, trying his best not to hurt her. She hit his face, but failed to loosen his grip.

Rick pulled her to the side, then pressed her against a tree. As he did, Atkins stepped up to Berente and aimed his pistol.

"Adios, *Frankenstein.*"

The jungle exploded behind him. Atkins whipped around and saw Danny, bleeding profusely through several gaping cracks in his exoskeleton. The one-eyed beast closed in and slashed his claw against his victim's chest, knocking him backward.

Rick released his grip on Ashley and backed away. He had no gun to fight with. Only a knife and a grenade, which at this range would also kill Atkins.

The mercenary scooted away from the beast, passing a triumphant Dr. Berente. He smiled, eagerly awaiting the spectacle of his creation destroying his sworn enemies.

"Yes! Good Danny! Do it! Kill those who have wronged you!"

Danny stopped, then tilted his head down at the doctor. Berente's smile disappeared. He saw anger in Danny's face.

The beast towered over him, his right hand still bleeding from the two missing fingers. That pain would end with time. The pain he felt from betrayal...that would only subside with retribution. He raised his claws to slash at the doctor.

"No! Danny!" Ashley screamed. She rushed toward her husband, waving her arms to get his attention.

"Ashley, no!" Rick called after her.

Danny turned toward her and snarled, hot breath carrying the odor of his countless victims. Ashley held her hands out and slowed.

"Danny. It's me," she said. She smiled. "You remember me? You remember our date at the Marine Corp Ball? Oh, come on, I know you haven't forgotten." She chuckled and moved closer, then reached out and grazed his body with her hands. "I missed you."

Danny slowed his breathing, seemingly mesmerized by his wife's touch.

"I know you've missed me," she said. She hoped he would speak. Berente had never mentioned whether he was able to communicate. It wouldn't matter soon anyway, as long as the good doctor remained alive to make good on his promise.

"We can have a whole new life together," she said. "You and me. We can live out here, free. The doctor can make that happen for us. You want that, don't you?"

There was no discernable emotion coming from the creature, other than intense breathing. Ashley smiled, her palms now pressed to Danny's rigid chest.

"I know you know me," she said. She reached back and peeled her tank top straps off her shoulders, revealing more of her cleavage. "I know you miss all of this. The times we used to have together. We can have them again. I love you, Danny."

Danny gazed at her, then directed his gaze at the man behind her. Rick Eilerman. The man she was unfaithful with. Danny growled like a rabid dog, his anger and violent instinct mixing into an explosive combination.

"Danny?" Ashley gasped. She stepped back and screamed, but could not escape his grasp. The beast snatched her off the ground and sank his teeth into her neck.

"Jesus," Rick muttered, witnessing his friend tear the flesh from his wife's neckline. Even Berente was horrified at the sight. He scooted backward, watching as Danny bit his wife a second and third time. Each attack shredded large masses of flesh from her. Her left shoulder was gone, her arm hanging by a few strands of meat. Her neckbone and chest plate were exposed, spilling rivers of blood. Yet, somehow, she was still alive. Her mouth opened to form words, but her vocals were gone. Danny redirected his attack to her midsection, ripping away intestines before splattering her corpse against the base of a tree.

Dripping with his wife's blood, Danny turned toward the retreating Berente.

"No, Danny!" he shouted. He tried to get up, but failed. With gaping jaws, Danny descended on the screaming doctor, skewering him with his claws. He pushed further until his fingers protruded out Berente's back. The doctor spasmed, then slowly gazed down to see Danny's left wrist disappearing into his stomach. His eyes remained there, oddly fascinated by the sight.

Teeth clamped down around his jugular, unleashing a scarlet fountain.

Atkins sprang to his feet, taking advantage of Danny's distraction to sprint to the hatch.

He turned the wheel and lifted it open, revealing a long climb down to a wooden dock. Rick ran as fast as he could, passing behind the creature, who had completed his execution by twisting his creator's head off his body. Danny whipped around, seeing his last two victims kneeling at the hatch.

"You go first," Atkins said. Not giving Rick time to argue, he pushed him into the hole, barely giving him a chance to grab hold of the ladder. The mercenary pointed his Beretta at Danny's mouth. "Nibble on this." Danny's head jolted back as the bullet struck his gums. He fired again, striking along the hybrid's face and neck, landing another bullet through his gill slits. The slide locked back. With no time to load another mag, Atkins descended into the hatch and slammed the door shut. He latched it shut, though it wouldn't do much to slow the beast, who would simply open it from the top.

Both men slid down the side rails all the way down to the dock. Boards rocked under their feet. They looked inward and saw several drums of fuel stored further in along the ledge, and a thirty-foot motorboat strung to the edge of the dock.

They hurried to it and climbed up onto the main deck. Atkins entered the cockpit. Luckily, the keys were in it. He started the engine, while Rick untied the line. To both of their surprise, Danny had not started climbing down. He didn't even open the hatch. It was odd, but he wasn't gonna stick around to ask questions. He throttled the boat out toward the mouth of the cave. There was only a hundred feet of distance to pass until they were out on the open ocean. He blew a sigh of relief as the sunlight touched the bow.

"Oh, yeah, we are outta here," he said.

A shadow fell over the bow, and like a meteor, Danny crashed down onto the cockpit. The windshield exploded, sending glass shards grazing Atkins' face. He fell face first onto the helm, accidentally putting the throttle in reverse. The boat slowed, then backed into the cave.

The hybrid wasted no time reaching his claw into the cockpit. Atkins fell backward, barely avoiding the reach of that claw. Frustrated, Danny reached further, stuffing his entire upper body through the broken windshield. He saw Atkins reload the pistol and extend it toward him. A swipe of his claw sent it flying through the starboard window. Atkins scooted back, only to bump his head into the back wall. Danny reached again, this time well within range.

Rick yanked the backdoor open and pulled Atkins out onto the deck. Danny snarled angrily, and pulled himself the rest of the way through the cockpit. He sprang to his feet and approached his victims. He tilted his head to see both of them with his one eye.

"Come on!" Rick said. He leapt over the transom onto the dock. Atkins sprinted, once again avoiding the creature's reach, and followed his companion. Shrieking, Danny dove into the water.

Waves crashed repeatedly, then settled into a near-flat surface.

"Shit," Rick whispered to himself. He wasn't used to fighting literal aquatic creatures capable of breathing underwater. With no air bubbles, there was no telling where Danny was. The two men branched out slowly to minimize the chances of them being grabbed at once. They watched through the space between the floorboards, unable to recognize anything.

Rick looked over at Atkins, then at the motorboat. It was still perfectly functional, despite the damage from Danny's fall.

"Psst!" Atkins looked over at him. Rick tilted his head to the boat.

Atkins leaned slightly, shooting him with a glare. *Are you crazy? He'll come right for me!* Rick shook his head, mouthing "No he won't." He cleared his voice, then spoke loudly.

"You know, she really missed you, Danny!"

Atkins shook his head in a futile attempt to persuade Rick from using himself as bait.

"She confided in me. We got together to share our feelings. I guess it went beyond that. I knew it was wrong, but I guess I couldn't stop myself from going back to her."

The floorboards underneath him exploded. Rick summersaulted, clearing Danny's outreached claw. The hybrid raked the deck with his hands, pulling himself up through the hole he had created.

Atkins groaned. Rick's plan, whatever it was, was now in motion. He dashed for the boat and jumped, landing over the railing. He groaned and cursed, feeling as though his ribs just caved into his stomach, but proceeded to pull himself the rest of the way onto the deck.

Danny was halfway up now. Rick backed up to the fuel drums, his hands tucked behind his back. In his palm was the grenade given to him by Healy.

"I'm sorry, man," Rick said. "I thought you were dead. We had to leave. I had to look out for the team. I guess, in the long run, that's what ultimately killed them."

Danny pulled himself up further. He was now standing.

Rick's eyes went to Atkins. He was gathering something on the deck…a rope. Tied to the end of it was a flotation lifebuoy. He twirled it like a lasso, then launched it out along the dock.

It hit one of the support beams, drawing Danny's attention.

Rick unpinned the grenade and let it drop.

"Sorry, man." He dove over the side and grabbed the lifebuoy. Atkins gunned the throttle, dragging Rick out through the mouth of the cave.

The grenade detonated, exploding the fuel barrels. A wave of fire swept Danny off his feet, landing him thirty feet backward. Residual explosions popped within the cave, sending some of the barrels flying up into the ceiling.

Even with the ringing in his ears, Danny could hear the crumbling of sediment. He stared straight up, seeing the roof of the cave burning with fuel. Then, it crumbled, then succumbed to its own weight. There was no time to cry out in agony, or even attempt escape. His last memory as a genetic hybrid mirrored the last one as a human, as a world of burning debris dropped from above.

Thousands of pounds of rock crushed Danny's body, splintering his shell to bits, squelching his organs. The deck collapsed under him, buried with Danny in his watery grave.

CHAPTER 28

"Ow, you dumb bastard," Atkins muttered.

"Quit being such a baby," Rick said. He guided the stitch thread through the laceration in Atkins' chest, gradually closing it. He had managed to take threads from his shirt to make a line, and straightened a fishhook for a needle. Atkins would probably need a tetanus shot, but considering what they'd just been through, he was sure the guy could handle it.

"So, what now?" Atkins said.

"Well... there should be enough fuel to get this puppy to the coast. We have a full tank and one spare fuel drum. It'll be close, but we can probably make it to California. There's a little bit of water in storage. And I still have a few rations leftover from our initial supplies."

"And, we can always fish," Atkins joked, looking at one of the poles.

"That we can," Rick grinned.

"But uh, that's not what I originally meant. What are you doing after this?"

Rick sighed. "I have no idea. Everyone I know is on that island. Life won't be the same."

"It won't," Atkins said. "All I can say is, not *all* your friends are on that island."

Rick nodded and looked into the eyes of his brother-in-arms. The two men slapped hands, locking grips with each other.

"Thanks, Angelo. Now..." he got up and went into the cockpit, "...let's get the hell out of here."

He steered the vessel north and sped for home.

SEVEREDPRESS

CHECK OUT OTHER GREAT DEEP SEA THRILLERS

PREHISTORIC BEASTS AND WHERE TO FIGHT THEM
by Hugo Navikov

IN THE DEPTHS, SOMETHING WAITS ...

Acclaimed film director Jake Bentneus pilots a custom submersible to the bottom of Challenger Deep in the Pacific, the deepest point of any ocean of Earth. But something lurks at the hot hydrothermal vents, a creature—a dinosaur—too big to exist.

Gigadon.

It not only exists, but it follows him, hungrily, back to the surface. Later, a barely living Bentneus offers a $1 billion prize to anyone who can find and kill the monster. His best bet is renowned ichthyopaleontologist Sean Muir, who had predicted adapted dinosaurs lived at the bottom of the ocean.

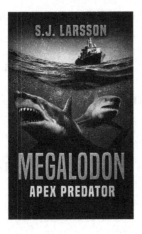

MEGALODON: APEX PREDATOR
by S.J. Larsson

English adventurer Sir Jeffery Mallory charters a ship for a top secret expedition to Antarctica. What starts out as a search and capture mission soon turns into a terrifying fight for survival as the crew come face to face with the fiercest ocean predator to have ever existed- Carcharodon Megalodon. Alone and with no hope of rescue the crew will need all their resources if they are to survive not only a 60 foot shark but also the harsh Antarctic conditions. Megalodon: Apex Predator is a deep-sea adventure filled with action, twists and savage prehistoric sharks.

 SEVERED**PRESS**

CHECK OUT OTHER GREAT
DEEP SEA THRILLERS

LOCH NESS REVENGE
by Hunter Shea

Deep in the murky waters of Loch Ness, the creature known as Nessie has returned. Twins Natalie and Austin McQueen watched in horror as their parents were devoured by the world's most infamous lake monster. Two decades later, it's their turn to hunt the legend. But what lurks in the Loch is not what they expected. Nessie is devouring everything in and around the Loch, and it's not alone. Hell has come to the Scottish Highlands. In a fierce battle between man and monster, the world may never be the same. Praise for THEY RISE : "Outrageous, balls to the wall...made me yearn for 3D glasses and a tub of popcorn, extra butter!" – The Eyes of Madness "A fast-paced, gore-heavy splatter fest of sharksploitation." The Werd "A rocket paced horror story. I enjoyed the hell out of this book." Shotgun Logic Reviews

TERROR FROM THE DEEP
by Alex Laybourne

When deep sea seismic activity cracks open a world hidden for millions of years, terrifying leviathans of the deep are unleashed to rampage off the coast of Mexico. Trapped on an island resort, MMA fighter Troy Deane leads a small group of survivors in the fight of their lives against pre-historic beasts long thought extinct. The terror from the deep has awoken, and it will take everything they have to conquer it.

CHECK OUT OTHER GREAT
DEEP SEA THRILLERS

HELL'S TEETH
by Paul Mannering

In the cold South Pacific waters off the coast of New Zealand, a team of divers and scientists are preparing for three days in a specially designed habitat 1300 feet below the surface.

In this alien and savage world, the mysterious great white sharks gather to hunt and to breed.

When the dive team's only link to the surface is destroyed, they find themselves in a desperate battle for survival. With the air running out, and no hope of rescue, they must use their wits to survive against sharks, each other, and a terrifying nightmare of legend.

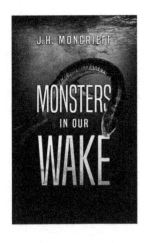

MONSTERS IN OUR WAKE
by J.H. Moncrieff

In the idyllic waters of the South Pacific lurks a dangerous and insatiable predator; a monster whose bloodlust and greed threatens the very survival of our planet...the oil industry. Thousands of miles from the nearest human settlement, deep on the ocean floor, ancient creatures have lived peacefully for millennia. But when an oil drill bursts through their lair, Nøkken attacks, damaging the drilling ship's engine and trapping the desperate crew. The longer the humans remain in Nøkken's territory, struggling to repair their ailing ship, the more confrontations occur between the two species. When the death toll rises, the crew turns on each other, and marine geologist Flora Duchovney realizes the scariest monsters aren't below the surface.